Black Rose Omen
Dark Ballads Vol 1.

Lexington, KY

This book is a work of fiction. Names, characters, places, and incidents are either the product of the author's imagination or are used fictitiously, and any resemblance to actual persons, living or dead, business establishments, events, or locales is entirely coincidental.

BLACK ROSE OMEN:
DARK BALLADS, VOL. 1

Copyright © 2024 Quiet Red Media

Editors:
Ali Lauderdale
Vanessa Anderson

Cover Art by Syadat Baihaqi
Interior Art by Imperial Skulls Studio, Jason Crager
Interior layout/typesetting by NightOwlFreelance.com

Paperback ISBN-13: 979-8-218-50986-6
Hardcover ISBN-13: 979-8-218-50982-8

CONTENTS

THE SHOWDOWN

BY QUIET RED

"*A bastard* of an old man, and he will punch a fiery hole through your skull for saying as much." This is how Master Yuen Zhāng Wei has been described among those who know his name. He's not a typical benign and wise old man, like you'd find among his peers. Master Wei is something quite different. He's certainly old, but Wei isn't one you'd turn to for advice or a sympathetic ear. In fact, most people avoid the old curmudgeon. His gritty ways have made him somewhat of a pariah, but they've also made him a prolific and masterful monster hunter. In his time as a hunter, he has garnered a certain amount of fame among men, and infamy among the rest.

His immense skill as a fighter is renowned and coveted, not just in his home country of China, but all around the world. Even his enemies must respect the mention of his name. The implausible and fantastic stories of his exploits have become a thing of legend. Indeed, there are those who can't bring themselves to believe the stories they've heard, but this tale is no legend. This is a recountal.

Master Wei was once a nomadic adventurer, scouring the world for challenges and battles to test his martial skill. Inevitably, this led him to the ever-present world of the supernatural, and after several public showings of might, Wei was regularly offered handsome sums for his skills. He began to take jobs as an enforcer and a hunter for those who were plagued by the paranormal. Anything that could be smacked in the mouth was subject to the bludgeoning force of his fists. In these times, he'd made plenty of enemies, but he'd also managed to make what could be called friends.

One of these friends, a fellow hunter named Jin Liu, had become embroiled in a situation in her village of Laimeng. Liu had come to the village years before to retire and live out the rest of her days in peace, having given up the life of a hunter long ago. She was alone, her family killed by vampires when her children were young.

Liu's life in Laimeng was simple, which was more than most could say in 1930s China. In a time of war and constant unrest, her golden years had been largely peaceful. The village was modest and rural, with a small enough population that everyone knew each other's name, as well as most of their business. And something had recently raised her attention.

Master Wei had, out of the blue, received a letter from Liu. Seeing as how Wei hadn't heard from her in quite a few years (twenty by his count), it caught his eye. However, Wei didn't open the letter. He placed it on a lacquer cabinet, just inside his doorway as soon as he saw who it was from, leaving it there, not opening it out of some semblance of the grudge the two were engaged in. The letter sat there for two days before the constant glances in its direction with each pass-by became as ridiculous to him as it would be to anyone else.

Feeling a bit foolish about the cold shoulder he'd so determinedly inflicted upon a small paper letter, Wei finally stopped with a final glance and walked over to the ornamental lacquer cabinet. Prying open the seal of the envelope, Wei's mind wandered between the moments of opening and reading, recalling the last vitriolic exchange of words between him and Liu. The two of them had fallen out over what seemed, in that moment, to be unworthy of the estrangement.

What he read was a plea; one that held an unmistakable tone of concern—almost frantic in nature. The letter stated that she suspected an interloper had infiltrated the village. She believed the creature to be a vampire and that it had potentially already turned several people in the community, as the population seemed to be increasingly dormant during the day and active at night. Her words conveyed an eerie sense of fear for both her life and those of the villagers.

Liu was asking for Wei to come to the village, and as he read the shakily scrawled parchment, he realized that Liu must feel backed against an insurmountable wall. Liu was no slouch in a fight. She could handle herself, but her old age must've caught up with her. She couldn't have anyone else to contact if she was asking him for help. Especially seeing as how their last interaction hadn't exactly been amicable. Sensing the fear in her words, Wei decided to answer her call and look into this, but Liu had specifically asked Wei to bring his students, fearing that the whole village could soon find themselves among the ranks of the undead. He had become "Master" Wei not long after they'd last seen each other, and apparently, she was aware. The problem was that his students were on a hunt, dealing with the emergence of a yaomo in Shanghai, a test of sorts, and one they couldn't break away from.

Wei would have to do this alone. And that he did. Just as spontaneously as he'd received the letter, Wei left for the village of Laimeng by himself. The journey was uneventful and tiring but nothing taxing. He arrived mid-morning, and taking cue from Liu's letter, found her home and let himself in. Liu wasn't there. Wei walked into the small humble home, closed the door and stood in the middle of the one and only room for a moment. He stood, taking in the smells, scanning the layout, and using the moment to think. He threw his travel sack across the room to a hook on the wall, hanging it perfectly as if carefully placed, then looked for some food. He helped himself to a modest meal, and after finishing it, sat directly in the middle of the room and began to meditate.

Wei sat completely still in a controlled trance until the fall of dusk. Not a soul appeared throughout the daylight hours. As nightfall approached and the evening sky settled into a sunless gloom, Wei rose and gathered his senses. When looking around the home, he'd already noticed there was no sign of a struggle. Since this was Liu's residence, that only left one option: she was taken while somewhere else.

Wei's presence had clearly riled the creatures in the village, and he could sense the wicked things squirming around outside, no doubt aware of his interloping. They could surely smell him, but Wei knew the rules. If they were indeed vampires, to which all indications point, they could not simply enter the home. Left only to skulk outside the thin walls of the modest structure, the creatures would need an invitation to enter.

Just as he'd expected, two shadowy figures stepped into the warm light of the lanterns in front of the home, one of them gently knocking on the door.

"Hello? We've brought you some fine youtiao. Mister?"

Wei was under no illusion; the two at the door were definitely not men. He could feel it. Their cold and breathless composure wasn't that of friendly neighbors, but that of inhuman scouts. At least they were trying, but no amount of fried bread could placate this particular old man. The two men knocked once more, this time a little harder. Wei was sitting at the sole table in the room, directly opposite the door, drinking a sub-par tea that Liu had on hand. *That's truly terrible tea, Liu,* he thought to himself, momentarily ignoring the two at the door. With an uninterested sigh, he placed the cup on the table and rose from the chair, adjusting his posture to portray old frailty. He strolled over to the door, shuffling his feet as he walked with the distinct leisure of an elder. Wei opened the door to the men and greeted them with a disarming demeanor indicative of a feeble old man.

One of them spoke through an unnatural grin, clearly trying to feign good intentions.

"Hello! You're new here, are you not? We noticed you'd come to our little village, but our manners had escaped us. We bring this as an apology for our oafishness."

"Yes, I arrived here only this morning," Wei responded with a stone-hard gaze. "Please, no apology necessary, young man."

The two scouts both dropped their shoulders slightly, looking reassured, if not a bit anxious, like a predator sensing the shallow breath of an injured prey.

"Very kind. May we come in?" A grim smile stretched across the face of the strange one speaking. The other, looking as if he was trying not to swat at a fly on his face. The two were trying their best to remain unassuming. A normal person may not have noticed it. Wei was no normal person.

"Why, of course, gentlemen. An old man like me would love to rattle your ears for a bit. I'd come here expecting to visit with my friend, but she seems to be gone for the time being. I've been resting my bones here in the interim." Waving the two men inside with a timid gesture, the lantern light from outside the door whisked the shadows across their faces as they crept inside. Wei knew the two would be set off if he alluded to knowing what they were. Regardless, the two lackeys posed no threat to him, and he'd done enough to substantially lower their guards. They were in for a rude awakening. But before that, he wished to get a little more information, hoping they were the chatty type.

As the two men settled in the center of the room, Wei shuffled to the teapot. "Please, have some tea. I'm sure it's not the best, but I'm afraid it's all I can offer."

Neither of them answered. Wei could sense the energy shifting in the room, but he couldn't kill them yet. He needed to draw this out a bit more. As one of them took a step forward with what was surely malicious purpose, Wei snapped around, tea in hand, presenting a freshly poured cup. Attempting to disarm them for a moment, Wei broke into some friendly banter and gently forced the man to take the cup.

"Here you are, young man. So, do you two happen to know my friend, Liu? She lives here."

The man holding the cup hesitantly spoke to answer in an uncertain tone, clearly derailed by the old man's oblivious innocence. "U-uh, yes,

yes, we know Liu." He glanced to his cohort as if to urge him to alleviate the situation. "Uh, she's probably at the market square."

"The market? At this hour? Oh, I don't believe so. Maybe she is held up somewhere."

"Held up… yes, perhaps. Why don't we go look for her together? If you follow us—"

Wei cut him off. "She's a forgetful old goat. She probably forgot I was coming. Is there a hall for recreation in the village? Perhaps a game of Go?"

"No, I don't belie—"

Once again, Wei interrupted. "Oh, she must be with another friend of hers, then. Are you certain there's no Go played around here? She does love her Go."

"No, but allow us to help—"

Yet again Wei interrupted the man, who then looked visibly frustrated. "I'm sure she'll be back soon. I should wait here for her return." Wei was trying to irritate the stranger into giving him something in a way that only an annoying old man could.

The man spoke again, this time with an urging tone. "If you will follow us, I'm sure we can help you find her. It's no trouble. We'd be happy to help."

"Oh, thank you, young man, but I think I had better stay and wait in case she returns. An old man like myself can't waste time playing hide and seek, wondering about. My old bones need a clear direction these days."

Wei baited hard. Almost too hard, but he wanted the oaf to open up.

"You know what? I just remembered. There is a Go game being held not far from here. Just at the edge of the village. We can take you."

As the scout spoke, Wei fiddled with the teapot and other objects nearby, appearing busy, back turned, and briefly smirked to himself before wiping the smirk and turning to face the fiend. "Just at the edge of the village, you say?"

"Yes, not far at all."

"So, that's where your head rat is hiding?"

The two men visibly tightened up for a brief moment, their faces intent, eyebrows furrowed. Wei's patience began to break down. The pair wasn't chatty enough for the tactic to provide much more, and Wei was bored with hosting them. The information he'd gathered was enough for him to go on. At the edge of the village was the base of the mountains. Wei figured the master vampire must've been holed up there somewhere, perhaps in a cave. Wei's anger was getting the best of him at this point, and the two morons being in Liu's home was starting to bother him, anyway.

Wei shed his feeble demeanor, stood up straight and spoke firmly, "Is that where she is? Or maybe in one of the housings in the village? If you tell me now, I won't make you suffer. If you don't… I'll use you to send a message."

The tea drinker laughed with a brief chuckle, not with humor, but signaling amusement. The fiends quickly changed their false front and the one closest to Wei threw the teacup against the wall, shattering it. "We were going to take you there, anyway. Though it seems like you're looking for a fight. I don't think our master will mind us taking one decrepit old geezer for ourselves. So, come here, old man. We're both hungry!"

The tea drinker lunged forward, grabbing at Wei, but before he could extend his reach, Wei smashed his foot into the vampire's nose, breaking it and simultaneously grabbed the fiend's wrists, holding him in place. Toying with the other one, Wei turned to put the tea drinker between himself and the second vampire, jerking back and forth.

"Ack!… Get him!" The tea drinker shouted to his cohort, muffled under the pressure of Wei's shoe on his face. Before the other vampire could react, Wei switched with blinding speed and brought his other foot to the tea drinker's chest with a bludgeoning force, launching him into the second vampire and sending them both to the floor. Wei stood in front of them, still holding the tea drinker's arms. As the tea drinker howled in pain, the second one ran full-bore at Wei, hissing with murderous intent.

As the vampire approached, Wei slapped one of the tea drinker's arms across his face, not once, not twice, but a total of fourteen times in the blink of an eye. The vampire was wobbled, but not knocked down and slashed at Wei's throat with his filthy claws, whiffing as Wei effortlessly dodged. In return, and with not a moment passing between, Wei stuffed the other one of the tea drinker's arms into the vampire's mouth sideways and just as quickly shoved his own arm directly through its chest. The creature fell backward and hit the floor with a wet thump, quickly beginning to rot at an unnatural rate. All of this taking place within moments as the tea drinker was still writhing on the floor.

"Damn it. I should've done this outside." Wei walked over to the armless vampire, waving accusatory gestures. "If Liu is still alive, she's going to kill me for making a mess of this place. You see what you've done? You've spewed your rancid fluids all over her floor."

"Ugh—listen! I—I can take you to her, okay? I can help you find your friend."

"Oh, I'm not going to kill you, so quit rambling. I've got a job for you." Wei shuffled to his left a few paces, reached to grab a cloth from the table and wiped his hands of the residue left from the other one's chest. As he did so, the armless vampire attempted to spring to his feet and out the window, getting so far as leaping toward the windowpane. But in mid-air, Wei quickly spun around and clocked the vampire with an axe kick that sent him thudding back to the floor and groaning with pain.

"I haven't told you what I need of you. Don't be rude," Wei asserted, with a sardonic tinge.

"You're going to be ripped apart, human! My master is ancient and powerful beyond your comprehension!" Blood leaked from the vampire's mouth as he spoke, likely a symptom of internal trauma.

"Calm yourself, wretch. I know your master sent you to assimilate me. Since that hasn't quite worked out, I'm going to ask something of you. Remember what I said earlier? You will relay a message for me." As Wei spoke, he finished wiping his hands with the cloth and tossed it aside. Squatting down next to the injured vampire, Wei continued his demands.

"You will go back to your master, and you will tell it that you failed. You will tell it that I will not be turned into a slobbering lackey, such as yourself. You will tell it that when I have cleared this village of all other groveling, needle-toothed sycophants like you, I will come for it... and I will kill it." Wei stood slowly, continuing, "If I find that my friend has been turned and I have to kill her, or that she's been killed by your kind, I will make your master feel the sensation of fear for the first time in its wretched existence, right before I end it. Do you understand?"

The vampire displayed a blank expression on its blood-soaked face as its feet slid across the floor, seeking traction to sit upright.

"You don't know what you're doing, old man. I'll be back." The vampire scrambled to its feet and leaped out of the same window it had tried to escape from moments before. As Wei watched it fade into the darkness of the night, he began to unbutton his shirt to remove and change it. He'd now have to prepare for a real fight. The message would be clear, regardless of how it was delivered. The master would see Wei for the threat he was and would then attempt to be rid of him. This, Wei could be sure of. And when they came... they would die.

With his intentions made clear and the death threat relayed to the master vampire, Wei didn't have to wait long for the second welcome party to show up. After another short meditation, he could sense their presence. This time, though, it wasn't just a couple of scouts. This time the master sent the whole damn village, and that's exactly what he expected. They'd come to dispatch him to keep him from thwarting their master's assimilation of the area, and with Wei's show of skill, the master wouldn't take any chances. Wei was sated with more of the sub-par tea, along with a few decent biscuits and some ginseng from his travel sack. He took the time to change into a fresh shirt, which seemed almost silly since he was about to splatter himself with the innards of these creatures, but it was comfortable for the time being.

Outside the quaint village home, Wei could hear the vampires converging. This time, they weren't being sneaky. Anyone could hear the ruckus going on out there. Wei walked to the broken window, peering out into the shadow and umbra. The small village was especially dark, nestled within a valley, leaving the moonlight obstructed by the surrounding mountains. Most people in this situation would feel fear and worry, even hopelessness. Wei, however, felt a calm and warmth. In place of the ever-tightening death grip of anxiety and discomposure one would expect, Wei felt only harmony and an unmistakable rush of pre-combat excitement—a warm static sensation rushing through his chest and limbs, like a strong shot of baijiu. This was by far the most formidable challenge to his martial ability that he'd come up against, but he knew that could be the case when he set off for Laimeng in the first place. He was ready for the challenge. What's more, he'd then have a new story to tell his students.

He was wearing his fresh silk shirt, with a traditional garb and a short-brimmed felt hat. Wei nonchalantly fiddled with the cuffs of his clean shirt and adjusted its fitting, grabbing it from the bottom and snapping the front of the shirt down with both hands. He walked out the front door, hands clasped behind his back, and stepped into the street, lit only by the lanterns in front of Liu's home. Not a single flicker of light was seen elsewhere in the village. Wei could feel the shadows watching. As they closed in on him, he looked around to behold a constellation of fiery orange pinholes from the vampires' night-adapted eyes, lancing the darkness all around him.

Wei, without hesitation, made his intentions known to the horde and their master. Speaking calmly, his words were ferried through the darkness by the cool night air. "You have a friend of mine. Face your death in the open, or in the shadows. You have a choice in that. But it ends tonight. In *this*, there is no choice."

The space around him resembled living shadows. The environment was writhing and wriggling and seemed to be moving in like a thick wave of cimmerian syrup.

Without warning, three figures manifested from the darkness and rushed Wei. He handily dispatched two with swift strikes that completely severed their heads. The third was faster than the other two and shot behind Wei, moving to grab him. Just before he obliterated its head with a powerful kick, sending a thick cloud of blood and bone into the air, more were already pouring from the murk.

Several tried to extinguish the lanterns, but Wei was swatting them away, like a swarm of moths to a literal flame, keeping a dim halo of orange light encircling him. He slayed anything that breached the line of illumination, quickly tearing through what must've been thirty vampires within the span of mere seconds as they continued to spill forth from the maw of darkness. The midnight vermin were undeterred by the rate at which their brethren were falling, their heads bursting like pumpkins struck with cannonballs.

Wei was in a blood-soaked dance of lightning-fast movement, the rubicund mist raining down and whipping inside a whirl of combat, held at a pace faster than normal human eyes could even begin to perceive. Limbs, heads, and other bodily pieces and entrails were spewing forth from the destructive vortex as Wei obliterated the creatures, like a rabid terrier descending upon rats. The battle was fierce, and the creatures were viciously quick, but Wei surpassed their speed and was far beyond them in skill.

His inhuman stamina was starting to pay off as he saw a noticeable dip in the volume of tooth and claw coming at his throat. The problem was that Wei had no idea how many people had been assimilated. The small village couldn't have been home to much more than two hundred or so villagers, but there was no way to know how many travelers and vagabonds had been collected. Wei knew he must've torn through over 150 rabid vampires at that point.

Finally, after dispatching one last tide of attackers, Wei stood alone among the pool of guts and chunks of rotting carcass, basking in the warm light of the lanterns, both still lit.

Wei walked over and took one of the rusty lanterns from the front of the house, then gathered his sense of direction. Aiming toward the south, he started to make his walk to the edge of the village before being confronted with a deafening wail. Wei stopped, looked ahead, holding the lantern eye level, and saw a hulking figure step slowly into the light.

Wei felt every step rumble under his feet as the creature plodded a few steps closer, becoming fully visible in the lantern's glow. Standing before Wei was a massive creature stained with blood, dirt, and the remnants of whatever he'd devoured over the course of what looked to be a very long time. Its bottom jaw jutted forward, revealing gnarled, sharp yellow teeth and profuse slobber dripping from its stone-carved chin. The creature was presumably a vampire but wasn't the typical sort, standing about seven and a half feet tall, not accounting for its hunch. It appeared to be some sort of mutt, covered in scars and asymmetric features. Wei sized up the mountainous vampire without any change in demeanor, completely unresponsive to the beast's visage.

From behind the large creature, Wei heard an irritating cackle ringing through the air. Stepping out from the shadow of the beast was the armless vampire Wei had confronted earlier. The smug look on his face was every indication of the craven little devil's assumption of the situation. Obviously, the mutilated worm thought he'd become the harbinger of Wei's demise. As Wei stood with a stoic, if not slightly bored, look upon his face, the armless vampire began to taunt him in a shrill, manic tone.

"Where do you think you're going, geezer? You can't possibly have thought it would be that easy. I told you I'd be back! And I brought company. Get ready to swallow your empty words, you tired old shit!"

Cackling loudly between each pause, the vampire continued with ever-increasing intensity, "My friend here is not just another turned villager for you to slaughter! I have shepherded your death! You will pay for what you did to me and die in the street, where you stan—"

As the annoying posturing of the vampire reached the point of being unbearable, the large mutt suddenly slapped his palm atop the babbling vampire's head mid-sentence. Wrapping its large fingers around his head, the mutt lifted the tea drinker up to its toothy mouth, dipping him in feet-first and biting into him at the stomach. As the tea drinker screamed in horror, the mutt tore the smaller vampire apart like a gristly steak and threw the leftovers at Wei's feet. Wei stared into the widened eyes of the ill-fated wretch at his feet, as the dim and unnatural light faded into black ocular voids. The large monster then lazily raised its arm to point at Wei and began to speak in a monstrous, unnatural voice.

"You, old man… You've been chosen. You will be my meal. Master has allowed me from my cage to feast upon you."

Wei stood with a blank expression on his face, sighed and uttered, "Huh… you can speak. Wasn't expecting that. I guess I should thank you for shutting him up." The behemoth looked perturbed and tilted his head.

"I can speak. I can eat. I will eat you. I like you, gray one, for I have been let out to feast upon you. I will eat you quickly." The mutt plodded toward Wei, breathing heavily.

"Well, you're not the most well spoken I've come across, but it's certainly amusing. Alright, big guy. Let's get this over with."

The large monster exploded with speed and swiped at Wei, almost catching him off guard. The mutt's speed was noteworthy for such a hefty figure. Wei slid backward as the beast followed suit. The mutt stomped at Wei, slashed, swung, and punched, trying to catch him, but Wei was too sharp and too fast. The beast couldn't catch up to Wei and took a heavy strike to the ribs that broke several of them. Unaffected, the mutt attempted to backhand the old man, missing and taking a hard counter to the same ribs, destroying the rest of them and turning its rib cage into pulp. The monster roared and managed to actually connect with a fast punch. Even though he blocked it, the blow knocks Wei back, his feet sliding over the dirt.

The two squared off once more and briefly stared each other down before engaging again at a furious pace. Hundreds of strikes were thrown between the two before, at last, the mutt became sloppy and lingered a bit too long, which is all Wei needed. He leaped over a punch, ran up the beast's arm and kicked its head clear from its hulking body. Wei stood on its shoulders and rode it as it fell to the ground with a tremendous wallop. Wei hopped clear over the blood spilling from the mutt's neck and walked toward the edge of the village, still holding the lantern in his hand.

Wei knew he was in the master's lair as soon as he stepped through the makeshift archway leading to the vampire's chamber. The unmistakable stench of death, both fresh and days past, a tinge of iron in the air. The smell grabbed him like a firm ligature, but he'd experienced the revolting sensation enough times that he didn't reel or react with anything but the clinch of his jaw. It was simply a sign that he was in the right place.

Wei made his way deeper into the dank, foul-smelling lair with a calm stride, lacking any semblance of caution at all. He knew the creature could already smell his blood. There was no use in stealth. At any rate, all the expired vampires burned into the streets outside had surely marked his presence well enough. Wei could hear the frantic, disordered rustling of the creature as he reached the penultimate bend in the corridor.

Stepping into the dead end, immediately visible through the dim lighting shone from his lantern was the undead figure, resembling a dark and jagged bipedal silhouette, something akin to a weathered scarecrow twitching erratically in a soft breeze.

The disgusting vampire was looming menacingly a short distance from Liu, who lay inanimate on the cold cave floor. Wei gently set down the lantern, creating an intimate, if not haunting, atmosphere, and stepped forward to confront the filth-covered creature. As he stared into the vampire's milky dead eyes, his mind focused in a way that would seem unattainable to a normal man. He saw every ripple of flesh, every sinew of muscle and every change of stance or posture, in anticipation of even the slightest of movements and bodily exertion.

The creature was wiry and lean, but visibly strong. It was completely hairless and filthy, like mangy vermin. The vampire's body was covered in irregular bony shapes and its ribs were unnaturally large, with oddly long limbs and fingers. Its teeth were visible through the receded selvages serving as lips. All these things point to what was indeed a very long-lived vampire, time and evil having twisted its vessel beyond human bounds. Its bald head was sufficiently grimy that it barely reflected the light. Its teeth, however, glistened with saliva and vicious intent.

The master found it amusing that this mortal man would be so unwitting to just brazenly waltz into his beautifully grisly, gore-covered chamber. Wei's skill was obvious, but... still. Ancient vampires were far more than leagues beyond simple progeny. The creature wondered if the man was senile, stupid, or just oblivious. He was, in fact, none of these. The master vampire was simply ignorant of the skill that it was up against.

In a hissing, uneasy tone, the vampire spoke. "You're here just in time to witness this hunter's flesh peeled from her bones. Excellent timing. The display shall be... exquisite."

He knows Liu is a hunter, Wei thought to himself, *She must've shown her hand, somehow and gotten herself caught.*

Wei could hear the blood-coated phlegm rattling in the back of its throat as it spoke. "I've never understood your kind. The arrogance and self-importance are baffling to me. I've found much of nothing to redeem the human race in my eyes. The only true virtue of your breed is your insignificance—how you simply fade away and unburden the world of your existence—the lack of permanence... the finality. Shall I show you what I mean?"

"Is this part of your big plan? Skinning innocent old ladies and waxing poetic? Seems like a lack of ambition, really. I'm honestly disappointed."

"There's no need to be disappointed, dear mortal. You've caught only a glimpse of the abyssal majesty I shall rain down upon this world! I wouldn't expect your mortal mind to comprehend." The vampire clenched its blood encrusted fist and lowered its tone to a menacing grumble. "However, you've put quite a dent in my numbers in this area. For that, I shall rend you in pieces. That is all you need concern yourself with. First though, allow me to finish playing with my food." The sound of its voice was harsh and ferocious, aiming to frighten the old man. It failed.

As the bony fiend slowly approached Liu, Wei, in a blur of movement, stepped into the vampire's path, defiant and confident.

The vampire was almost startled, but he laughed, amused, if not a bit unnerved. The vampire growled, "Ahh, so you've decided to die first. How heroic of you. First, I must ask: Who exactly is this brainless mortal maggot staring into my deadened eyes?"

"It's unnecessary for us to exchange pleasantries, vampire. You'll have no need for my name with soup pouring from your skull," Wei responded. His irreverence to the situation, palpable.

"Indeed," the vampire quipped. "I suppose you'd like to stop me from plucking the wings from this insect, yes? That's what this little standoff is about?"

Wei smiled and mimicked the creature. "Indeed."

The vampire was no longer amused, and the sadistic smirk quickly faded from his gaunt, angular face.

Hiding the burgeoning uncertainty in his raspy voice, the master vampire became visibly angry. With an uncollected, almost blurting delivery, he shouted, "I think I'm done with this little show of arrogance from you, mortal! Step aside."

The vampire took two steps, attempting to knock Wei aside. As he did, Wei countered ferociously with a combination that dropped the stunned vampire, knocking him on his back.

The sound of the creature hitting the ground echoed off the cave walls with a satisfying reverberation.

"Ungh!…Well, I'll be damned. The little human has a bite of his own."

"As I understand it, you're already damned. I'm just here to expedite the process. Now, I'm old and I'm tired. Can we get on with it?" Wei didn't try to hide his utter boredom and disinterest in the circumstances.

"Right… how very amusing. Many thanks for the lesson in patience," red stained spittle whirled from his thin cracked lips as he aggressively hurled words from his mouth and stood back up, "…but I am no longer amused, human. Step aside now and I won't pull your lungs through your chest."

The vampire tried its hardest to instill a sense of dread in the old man as it rose to its feet, almost preoccupied with doing so, but Wei hadn't moved a muscle since knocking the vampire down and showed not so much as a hint of fear, nor worry. Wei's eyes simply locked with the vampire's and coldly followed them as he stood. His breath was steady, and the vampire noticed. And Wei noticed that it noticed.

"As much as I'd like to oblige, especially seeing as how you've asked so nicely, I think I'll stay right where I am, between her and you. Now, shall we see what you're made of?" Wei's impatience showed as he got into stance, the thin soles of his shoes sliding across the grains of dirt and viscera on the floor, his body relaxed but taut. The vampire saw that this aged human was not looking to talk or run and there was a clear sense of tension in the air, mixed in with the iron and rot.

The vampire was almost shocked and clearly unhappy about the show of defiance. "Enough! You want to see what I'm made of? So be it!"

It let out an otherworldly sound, something between a viper's hiss and the roar of a buffalo, and rushed in attack. Wei again countered, the vampire's hasty aggression used against him as Wei flung him a good 10 feet away. He landed on his feet, turning with blistering speed, but Wei had already closed the gap and was well within striking distance of him. It happened so fast the vampire didn't even have time to be surprised. The creature was quickly peppered with a vicious flurry of punches, kicks, and elbows, once more striking at a rate that would look like nothing more than a bothersome floater in the eye to a normal human. The two battled toe-to-toe, both standing their ground and fighting so hard that the air warmed around them. Eventually, the vampire was outmatched by Wei's sheer martial ability and staggered with hard blows. The vampire was rattled, gritting its teeth and, out of instinct, attempted to subdue Wei with its raw strength, but was unable to get a grip on Wei because of the old man's fluid movement and avoidance. It was pure skill keeping Wei on top.

The vampire was discombobulated and unprepared for this situation, getting its tooth knocked out and nearly being rendered unconscious by the human's sledgehammer-like blows. It could barely understand the situation it was in. Centuries of existence and never had this being been subjected to an assault quite like this, let alone from a mortal man—an elderly mortal man, at that. It dashed backward through the air with supernatural agility to regroup, but Wei stood fearless and unflinching, not a glimmer of sweat nor a single heavy breath to be found.

Wei could see the creature's nerves unraveling in fear and befuddlement. The old man was something otherworldly. This was no normal human. This was a legend.

Standing firmly, twisting the ball of his foot into the dirt, Wei mused antagonistically, "Something wrong, friend? Can you not best a mere man in combat? I suppose I did you a favor by dispatching your progeny. Nobody's here to see you die."

The vampire, frustrated, felt a rare and intensifying sense of fear and saw that this human may be too risky to clash with at the moment. Its plans were already foiled, and its progeny was no more than litter in the streets, soon to be decay and dust. This old man had thoroughly ruined the vampire's plans. So, with a wrenching ball of inner turmoil in its gut, the vampire waffled with pride and terror, ultimately deciding to retreat in anger.

Wei stood across from the vampire, still and calm. His intentions, like his thoughts, were completely unreadable. But the vampire knew that the old man's goal was to stamp this encounter with a finish. The vampire's countenance was far less effective, and Wei could see that it was looking for an escape.

The vampire looked at the floor, then its eyes moved up to focus, not on Wei, but looking past him, to the exit. The moments that passed seemed to go on for an eternity. And that was plenty of time to focus one's chi, something the vampire couldn't perceive and was in fact the source of power in the blows this human delivered. Indeed, he was no normal man, but a master of his spiritual energy. A practiced and skilled warrior that could put his stiffened fingers through folded steel and pick a leaden bullet from the air at any range. Even as a man in his seventies, his chi mastery was a talent that made him effectively supernatural in capability.

Finally, after an eternity had passed, in a low, defeated tone the vampire hissed, "This is far from over, *rrrat*. I will see your innards dangling between my fingers soon enough. Enjoy this fleeting victory while you can."

The stale cave air was quickly riled when the creature suddenly burst into a breakneck sprint, the force of his launch kicking up a plume of dust and debris. As the vampire attempted to barrel past Wei to flee the cave, Wei suddenly broke stillness with explosive speed and caught the vampire with a tremendous and perfectly timed blow to the head. The strike shattered the creature's skull, splattering the walls with the contents of his head, and dropping him to the floor. The vampire's momentum carried his limp corpse into the wall ahead of him, sliding to a sudden violent thud.

Wei calmly snapped the cuff of his right sleeve and subtly stroked the fine silk for a moment. He stood, facing the wall, with a blank expression and a melancholic gaze into nothingness permeating his face as he fiddled with his sleeve. As his focus settled back in, he looked at Liu's body out of the corner of his eye, without moving his head. He paused for another moment before slowly turning toward Liu, who still lay motionless on the floor. Placing his hands behind his back, he peacefully walked the few paces to her body. She was completely still, not breathing. He drew in a deep breath and exhaled with control and dolefulness.

Liu was lifeless. He'd felt it when he first walked into the vampire's chamber. Her aura was gone. For a moment Wei's mind wandered, thinking of a reality where he'd shown up in time. If he'd *used* those two loathsome days spent stubbornly avoiding her cry for help... If he'd only opened the letter when he received it... but he hadn't, and she laid dead because of it. A meaningless twenty-year grudge over a disagreement in philosophy having cut her life short.

But all of the pain, all of the regret, all of the guilt... it changed nothing. Her last days of peace and solace were robbed. No less, by one of the very things that killed her young family... and that's that. His vengeance on the creature meaning little to nothing in the grand scheme of things—if there was such a thing. Its limp mutilated corpse and the dark chunks of coagulated blood left on the cave wall provided no consolation to him. The best he could do was give Liu a proper burial and show her the respect she deserved. She was a true hunter, a mother, a wife, a friend. That *thing* didn't deserve to kill her.

Wei smiled through the pain and guilt for a moment as he wondered how surprised they were by the fight she must've put up. The old gal always was a fighter. Wei knelt to scoop her up in his arms and walked out of the chamber.

"Lets go see your family, Liu."

ROCKICIDE
BY VON KLAUS

"This ain't rock n' roll. This is genocide."
— *David Bowie*

His eyes shone black, and his mouth grinned with raw meat redness as he held the massive pills out to them.

"Communion before we go on," Nick Haven said.

But Nick wasn't Nick anymore. His face was smudged with white paint and black grease, streaking into a frightening form. Blood smeared across his teeth, rendering them coppery red. It wasn't makeup. It was transformation into... *him*. His other self.

The Hunter.

The most controversial unholy rock n' roll sex god to ever make an arena roar. The one that has to go out on stage and face down the audience can't be Nick.

Nick was too passive. Nick left tender kisses on the foreheads of sleeping hotel groupies. The Hunter was his unleashed opposite. The Hunter leaves scars on the faces of passed out groupies and they thank him for it later. A sick animal inside of Nick took over for performing, and when we say perform, we mean: scare the hell out of everyone and make a fuckton of money doing so.

His bandmates reminded themselves of said fuckton as they watched him standing shirtless amongst glittering shards of mirrors from the trashed dressing room. Each silently stared down at the pills in his filthy palm. All of them knowing: The Hunter gets what he wants, one vicious way or another.

"Yeah, sure thing," said Dimi, guitar over his shoulder. Dimi was always *first*. He was Nick's longtime friend and had formed the band with the guy as kids. And still... it was clear that Dimi was scared to death of The Hunter. He loved Nick the same way a beaten child loves their parent: cautiously. His palm opened with that caution for a pill.

The Hunter instead placed the pill upon Dimi's lips and waited for him to open up and accept the shining capsule. Trev looked at the Hunter, then down at the pills in his hand, then back up. Trev had thought he would be the party guy in the group. He'd thought he'd seen it all.

He had never seen The Hunter.

"Fuck it," Trev belted while grabbing a pill and downing it with a deep pull of whiskey.

"There we go! We win with chemicals, just like them star athletes," The Hunter said with a wide red grin as the shrieks of the crowd and their stomping feet boomed around them. "Time to go on."

Dimi wanted to tell Nick that he was afraid. Afraid the rock life was catching up with them; they all expected to find Nick dead at any moment. That he was feeling like a shadow was eating him alive. Instead, he just nodded and tightened his mouth as he always did, hoping to god the pill he just took didn't kill him.

The pills were already kicking in by the time they got to the stage. The audience roared like hungry cannibals at their prey. The Hunter roared back.

The music swelled, harsh and distorted over the arena. A wave of fans, their faces painted up like The Hunter's, reached for the stage as if for life itself. The distortion rose higher still, becoming a hum of the rage to come, vibrating through the audience, drowning out their shouts and filling their spines with resounding ominous intent.

The Hunter gazed back at the sea of faces like his staring back.

They all felt his *look* move through them. A mass of bodies there to worship his every move. They all shrieked like banshees as he twisted his hands around the microphone and pressed his black lips against its metallic covering.

"Are you ready? … You aren't ready. No one fucking is. You're not getting outta here alive, I can tell you that!"

Guitars rose to vengeful wails, crashing and drowning the audience in savage noise.

Trev's drums thundered through their hearts in the dark, smacking them with sonic death. The arena soared with screaming, writhing bodies soaked in firelight from the stage explosions, mad with worship as if at some sweaty ancient ritual. The Hunter grinned as he stared down his fitting audience.

Let the ritual commence.

It was there that the music left The Hunter's ears. Was it the droning of doing the same songs every night on a 3-year tour? No. Was his hearing finally blasting out of his skull? No. There was only a heartbeat bursting in his ears as the audience slowed their movement. Their arms dropped. Their faces fell blank. What the hell were they looking at? Did they forget who their master was?

Their faces shifted in the blackness as they grinned at The Hunter with his patented bloody grin. The shadows moved across their faces, covering them in Hunter makeup. The crowd of Hunters smiled at him in the dark. And The Hunter smiled back.

"Is this what you want?" The Hunter said, grabbing one of the gleaming black guitars on stage. "Is it?!"

The Hunter smashed the guitar on the stage floor, shredding it at the neck. Fibers of wood sprayed across the stage, along with some guitar strings. He gripped the jagged hunk of guitar neck like a savage club.

"Is this what you want?"

The Hunters in the audience grinned wider.

The dark shifted around them, swallowing every wicked face until only one Hunter remained, staring through Nick from the black, silent arena.

Nick slammed the broken guitar into his neck, coating the audience in a spray of blood.

Four months later, Nick Haven held the largest press conference of his career. And the press couldn't stop yammering about what happened. They never missed a moment to sell the fear.

> *Shocking News: Controversial Rocker and Lead Singer of Slow Death, Nick Haven, Tried To Kill Himself On Stage!*
>
> *Crowds broke through the barriers, rushing the band.*
>
> *Dozens were trampled in the chaos. Bandmates discovered that the pills he gave them were overdoses. Their roadies, trained through experience, had to pump their stomachs backstage. Nick barely survived, leaving the world stunned and questioning the boundaries between reality and performance.*
>
> *Once the audience made it to the stage, Nick fell on them, bleeding out. Suicides and attempts followed in the audience soon after, along with a few rapes and murders. Nick's blood was found for sale online.*
>
> *Band-mates Dim March and Trev Holiday have dropped all charges but also commented that there was no "suicide pact."*
>
> *More at 7.*

Cameras chirped and crackled as Nick and Cassie Cain took their seats behind a wall of microphones. Nick was slumped into the large black coat and his over-sized sunglasses, hiding behind strands of black hair. Cassie was his longtime on-and-off girlfriend. Her platinum hair and beauty were undeniable, even when dressed down for the conference, though the wear of late rock n' roll nights showed on her skin. And there were the lines around her mouth, carved out of the tightness of worrying about Nick for nearly a decade.

"Yes, it's true. I'm retiring. Call it the death of a legend if you want in your headlines, but I have to have a life," Nick said shakily. "Cassie and I are engaged now, and we're happy to announce...uh..."

"I'm pregnant," Cassie said, flashing white teeth and gripping Nick's hand. The media gasped with joy as the cameras snapped their shutters wildly.

"Congratulations!" said a young reporter. "So a little Hunter is on the way?"

"No, I've never really been a fan of that name," Cassie quipped.

Laughter erupted from the press as Nick tuned them out from behind his shades, staring blankly as camera flashes bounced off of him. Still, the reporters dug like vultures.

"Did overcoming suicide and this baby on the way help you to-"

"I didn't overcome anything," Nick said with heat, leaning into the microphones. "It will always be there. That's why I'm starting new with Cass."

Cassie smiled nervously, chuckling as the cameras chirped and the flashes blinded them. Nick fell back into his seat. He was rubbing his thumb down one of the lines on his arms, and by this point, a scar that had gone down the entirety of his forearm.

"So going forward, we'd really appreciate it if you could just give me and my family peace," Nick said wearily. "Just let us leave this world behind us already. Thank you all for your time."

Their new house was a modern-style masterpiece built by some mad architect wanting to get away from it all. Hidden away in the forest recesses of Connecticut, its wood construction and stone gave off a soothing, natural scent and its cool concrete floors comforted the feet to the touch. Floor to ceiling windows throughout the house showcased the surrounding red maples.

Dead of night, and Nick hadn't fallen asleep. He spooned Cassie, rubbing her belly softly, before sliding his thin frame out of bed so as not to wake her.

The fridge light blazed into Nick's eyes before he realized he was opening it for no real reason. He closed it, once again darkening the room, when he saw it: a small, pale face in the moonlight, just by the trees, watching him.

Nick rubbed his eyes and looked again. There it was, wearing the makeup he knew too well. The Hunter's face. Same grin as ever.

KER-SHOK! The pump of the shotgun rang loudly through the backyard, echoing into the shadowy trees ahead. Nick raised it and stood ready.

"Ok, super fan. You have 3 seconds to fuck off, or I'll come in shooting. You hear me? Let's hear those fucking-off sounds, now!"

A sliver of light elsewhere caught Nick's eye. He saw The Hunter standing by the sliding door to his bedroom with Cassie, the door cracked open. He grinned at Nick from across the yard, his teeth gleaming. The hunter slid through the curtained opening, pulled the door closed behind him.

Nick felt his lungs burn as he rushed across the yard to them. "Cass! CASS!"

Nick yanked the door open and pushed through the curtain to find the bedroom dark. No light. Nick aimed the gun as he scanned the room, sweat beading into his eyes. No sight of The Hunter, just Cassie propped up on an elbow, eyes wide, her hand out in fear.

"Did you see him?!" Nick rattled.

"No, babe. I didn't see anyone. Please. You're scaring me."

Nick lowered the gun slowly, breathing heavily, now drowning in sweat. "He was painted up like..."

Cassie took Nick's hand and placed it on her swollen belly.

"We're fine, see?" Cassie said tenderly. "Shh. Bad dreams happen. Especially when a lot changes all at once, babe."

Nick sat on the edge of the bed all night as Cassie slept. He sat until he felt the warm tap of the sun poking through the curtains on his shoulders and the shadows were gone.

Nick had to get out. He shoved the keys into his 1970 Chevelle SS and let the *vroom* of the engine pulse through him. The road spiraled through the red wood trees, turning into railed cliffs and man-made tunnels cutting through the mountainside. Nick had driven through these tunnels countless times, but something about them had changed. The shadows, the air, the sounds, and even time all seem to go still for a second before reaching sunlight again.

A new tunnel swallowed Nick, the orange lights of it blinking around him before going completely dark. The pinpoint of daylight at the tunnel's end was gone. Nick didn't believe it for a moment. There was no end. Nick popped on his headlights as a black figure slid across his rearview mirror. He looked back. Nothing.

He felt the figure watching him, now in the passenger seat.

"Do you not like me anymore, Nick?" The Hunter said in his rasping voice.

Nick didn't want to look, but he did. The Hunter's horrid death makeup and animalistic eyes grinned at Nick, teeth coppery with blood. He sat quite comfortably in the leather seat, completely focused on Nick.

"You know what I miss that I bet *you* miss?" The Hunter jabbed. "Driving."

"Not really," Nick said, as he tried to look back on the road that wasn't there in the dark.

"We used to have fun. You sure?"

A heavy chill filled Nick and he couldn't tell if it was fear or just the icy staleness of an undead creature sitting in the car next to him. "What are you?" Nick asked in the dark.

"I'm you at your best, and you know it," The Hunter replied.

"You tried to kill me."

"No, *you* tried to kill *us*, Nick."

Nick felt his eyes close, and in a blink he was in the passenger seat, and The Hunter was at the wheel, still leering and grinning at him like a madman.

"There we go!" The Hunter belted while slamming his foot to the accelerator. They tore through tunnel after tunnel, weaving between car after car, screeching over cliff-side edges. Nick didn't scream. He held on for dear life inside, watching his life pass before his eyes over and over as he looked over the edges of the road to the rocky beaches below. He felt his sweat raining down over his cold skin as the smell of burning tires and exhaust shocked his senses. Over the engine's *vrooms* and tire's banshee wails, Nick could hear The Hunter's laughter.

The Hunter turned into another tunnel, slamming Nick into the door. Nick regained his balance enough to slap a hand on the Hunter's shoulder.

"You... aren't driving. I am. You hear me?! *I* am!"

The Hunter grinned at Nick and with a slide of the wheel, headlights flooded the cabin. A truck horn roared through them as the lights became blinding. Another blink, and Nick felt the wheel in his hands again. He spun the wheel just as a massive 12-wheel semi barreled past them. He could still hear its horn as the tunnel ended. Nick pulled over just as the sunlight hit him again.

He hadn't noticed his breathing, but as the car stopped, he could hear himself gasping for air. No amount helped. The Hunter was gone. Nick stepped outside of the car and clung to the guard rail, trembling as he gasped.

It was raining that night when Nick's ex-band-mates arrived at Raven's Bar.

Raven's was just as dingy and dive-y as ever, and the funk of years of smoke and spilled beer seeped off the wood. It was a smell that comforted Nick and his band through faded memories. It was the smell of the morning when they'd decided to first become a band after downing whiskey all night. It was their temple, or in today's case, neutral ground.

Dimi and Trev entered; hands in leather jackets, sunglasses on. Nick waited for them in one of the more ratty booths and waved them over from across the bar.

"Hi-ya, Nick," Dimi said softly as he took a seat in the booth.

"Why are we here, man?" Trev tore straight to the point.

"First, I want to thank you both for coming. I wouldn't blame you if you didn't want to be around me much... after what I did," Nick said. "I wanted to tell you that I'm sorry."

Dimi and Trev both couldn't believe what they were hearing, and it showed on their faces.

"Alright, Nick. What's done is done," Dimi said first, breaking the silent weight. "We can move on."

"I thought you were bringing us out to Raven's to ask us to be a band again..." Trev said, deflated.

"No. Just wanted to say sorry to my old friends."

Soon after, the men were clinking their glasses and talking wild times on tour. The drinks poured, and the laughter flowed.

"You sure you don't want to shock the world and get Slow Death back together, Nick?" Trev said, pouring another round of shots. Nick silently looked down at the table.

"I can't. The Hunter needs to stay dead. Or else I'm dead too. You get me?" Nick said, as soberly as he could. "We're burying The Hunter tonight." Nick raised a glass, which the men tapped with theirs.

"Another round for my favorite band of all time!" said a sultry, cigarette-stained voice from behind them. It was Sheena Noxx, platinum-haired mega-groupie, and the owner of Raven's.

"Thanks, Sheena, but we're not a band. We just toasted to that," Nick said.

"Maybe just for tonight?" Sheena said with a grin, as she laid beers on the table, curving her vinyl coated body in all the ways she knew drove men crazy.

Dimi and Trev took up the beers, and Trev pulled Sheena to his lap. The tension was gone, and the party could finally ensue. For Nick, it was like being under water—the sounds, the sights, all a muffled blur around him. There was no celebration for Nick, only more and more drinks, as his friends slipped to the bathroom with Sheena to snort coke. The bar was closing up, and as the last people waded out into the rain, the lights were finally shut off.

Nick was too gone to drive and too tired to enjoy it. He laid back, and his eyes fluttered closed. As they did, a black-clad figure waved at Nick from the shadows.

"Fuck you. I won," Nick muttered as he passed out.

The hell of the morning hangover came on as sunlight pierced through Raven's barred windows and on to the face of Nick Haven. The smell hit him soon after—a hot, raw, coppery funk. Nick sat up in the booth. The bar was dark and empty, but something else was there. The blurriness gave way to hanging shadows. Almost like party decorations...

His band-mates dangled from nooses over the bar. Nick's shoulder brushed against the bony arm of Sheena Noxx. He turned to her. Her head was gone. Just the bloody stump of her neck remained. Nick noticed the blood on his own hands and tried to instinctively rub it away in panic as he shuffled out of the booth.

"Looks like ol' Sheena has given her last head," a rasp voice chuckled before Sheena's head rolled down the bar and landed, with blank eyes looking up at Nick.

"I thought you said these guys could party," The Hunter said while leaping to the bar between two hanging bodies. The bodies of Dimi and Trev dangled, purple faced with the bloat of death. He showcased them like a mad circus ringleader.

"You wouldn't *believe* how easy it was for them to let me in... but as you can see, they couldn't handle one night of *real* rock n' roll. We were always too good for 'em."

Nick pulled his phone out of his jacket. Dead. The Hunter laughed. "Can you blame me, Nick? You keep rejecting me, so I have to go somewhere else."

"But you *are* me," Nick belted.

"Not anymore. Now I'm free, and if I can't have you, I'll have the next best thing." Nick rushed from the bar as The Hunter's hoarse laughs echoed behind him.

Nick screamed Cassie's name before even getting through the door at home. No response.

Nick found a note quickly scribbled on the kitchen table. "Having baby. Where are you?"

Nick's messages blew up the second his phone regained charge. Cassie had gone into early labor. Nick showered off the blood with trembling hands and slid on fresh clothes. He was on full autopilot to Cassie and his child.

A sterile smell mixed with the faint scent of death hit Nick as he snagged flowers in the hospital gift shop. A sour-faced woman, seemingly in slow motion, greeted him at the check-in with a tired glance.

"Hi. My wife's in labor here. Last name: Haven."

The desk clerk climbed out of her coma, her eyes widening. "Oh. Yes, you can sign in, but you can't see your wife yet, Mr. Haven."

No.

"She's currently in surgery with complications."

No.

"The doctors will be out to see you shortly."

No.

Without saying a word, Nick walked directly to the bathroom he saw nearby. The lights flickered almost in greeting, getting no reaction from Nick. He found his reflection in the mirror over a row of sinks.

"Alright, you win. Let's set up a tour. One to honor the guys. Then you get me for the final show."

His reflection contorted in the mirror into the painted death that was The Hunter.

Doctors came to Nick to explain everything, which passed right over him as they rode up the elevator. Nick rushed to Cassie's room as the doctors lagged behind. She was drenched in sweat, red-faced, and gorgeous as ever, with a tiny bundle resting in her arms.

Nick fell to his knees and laid the flowers on her lap. His face fell into the soft warmth of the blankets, and he reached up towards the bundle to feel warm tiny fingers grip his index. He finally cracked. Nick wept and told them how sorry he was. How he would be better for them both. Cassie's voice rang softly yet sharply. "Where were you?"

"Trev and Dimi... I was with them last night. I tried to put the old band to rest. I thought it would help. Cass, when I woke up, they were dead. They'd hanged themselves..."

> *After the double suicide and murder trial that rocked the nation, Nick Haven is back and going on tour to honor his fallen bandmates. Fans are buying tickets in record numbers; however, Nick said he would be retiring his on-stage persona that gave him household recognition and controversy, and instead he will be, and I quote, "performing as himself."*

THE AGREEMENT
BY CLINT STOKER

The pain in Bailey's backside became just a brief distraction. Sure, she had the entire back seat of the car to herself, but if she was going to get a word in, she needed to ride the middle-of-the-seat hump all the way up the canyon. Every bump and curve of the crumbling canyon road became another nagging reminder of how awkward it all was. She hadn't paid much or any attention to the mountain scenery, not while Rob and Jude were holding hands, right in front of her, across the center console.

Rob clumsily navigated the winding road with his left hand while Jude flipped the visor down and examined her eyebrows in the mirror. They could have just held hands like a normal couple, but Jude caressed his fingers and traced his palm. Maybe it was just the newness of the relationship or a nervous tic. Either way, Bailey was starting to feel carsick.

Jude droned on about her approach to makeup, which was a surprise. Her porcelain face and pale lashes hardly seemed intentional.

Bailey leaned forward, ready to interject at any moment, but Jude didn't even pause to breathe.

"You think it'll rain, Robby?" Jude cawed. "If it rains... and here you are without your rain jacket..."

Rob remained stiff. "It won't rain."

She pulled her hand away and twisted in her seat to look at the clear, blue sky through the windshield for justification. "Sure, it doesn't look like it now, but if this is anything like Pike's Peak..."

Bailey found her opening. "You lost your rain jacket, Rob?"

"Yeah uh... Last time Jude and I went backpacking," Rob said.

"That sucks... And when did you say you climbed Pike's Peak, Jude?"

Jude looked back at the visor mirror. She wrinkled her nose and then checked her teeth.

"You two are cute," Jude said. "Almost like you have a little sister, Robby."

Rob seemed to hold his breath.

Bailey rolled back into her seat and failed to smother her groan. She glanced up at the rearview mirror to see the faintly desperate eyes of Rob looking back at her, begging.

A passing brown sign startled Bailey from the fleeting regret.

Bailey read it out loud, "High Uinta's Wilderness!" She barked, "Dude, we passed the trailhead a long time ago!"

Rob smiled thinly. "Slight change of plan," he said.

Bailey glared, but Rob just looked ahead at the road. Jude filled the awkward silence with an anecdote that Bailey could only tune out. The scenery started to look more familiar. Watching the road intently, Bailey wished it were anywhere else, but...

"This is it," Rob said.

The car slowed down at a small clearing by the side of the road, just beneath that old, familiar black boulder that sat at the edge of a rocky patch. The mountains split into a narrow canyon just beyond the black boulder, just like it looked in the pictures that Bailey had examined over and over again.

Bailey almost choked. "This is *the* trailhead. *The* hidden trail."

"Yeah." Rob's voice shrank, and he opened the door.

The trio got out of the car. Jude stretched her arms as Rob pointed proudly at the black rock. It's like he wanted it to mean something to her, but how could it? She hadn't been the one planning this hike for months. She hadn't heard the stories about the cold spring at the end or gone through all the trouble of keeping the spot secret, saving it for a special place to go when she wanted to be alone with Rob.

"I'm not kidding, Jude; this trail really is something special," he said. "Or that's what I hear."

"Oh, where'd you hear that, Rob?" Bailey opened the trunk and wrangled her pack out.

She whipped her pack around her shoulder and slammed the buckles together, so they each made a loud, frustrated *clack*. She marched toward the black boulder to join her *friend* and his lanky new girlfriend.

Rob lowered his head sheepishly, but he was not ashamed enough to let go of Jude's hand. Now that they stood outside of the car, it became obvious how much taller Jude was than Rob. Her long, flowing platinum hair only made her appear taller.

Jude squished her face and whipped her free hand at a cluster of mosquitoes that were pestering her. It was enough of a distraction for Rob to reach out and acknowledge Bailey.

"Listen, Bailey, I know we had planned to explore this trail together. That's why I really wanted to invite you to come along this weekend."

Bailey pulled on her pack straps, cinching them tightly. "That's right. *We* were going to explore this trail, weren't we?" She started off around the dark boulder, knowing Rob and Jude were watching her storm off. Her cheeks felt flush, and she wanted to turn and apologize for being a brat, but she'd settle for pretending nothing happened.

The trail barely started before it became nearly impossible to see the ground. Large-leafed foliage stretched across the path, each plant competing for the dappled sunlight that made it past the thick canopy above. Aspen trees broke through layers of green foliage with their slender, white-barked trunks. The air seemed to grow cooler by the minute. Soon an hour, then two, passed, and Bailey could see her breath as she silently led the march.

"Wait up, Bailey!" Rob shouted.

Bailey turned around to see Rob and Jude standing higher on the slope and on a clear trail. It was just a twenty-yard difference, but under normal circumstances, Bailey wouldn't have missed the turn. At least that's not how all of this had played out in her head before. She balled her hands into fists.

"I need to pee," Bailey lied, "go on ahead."

Rob hesitated. His face dropped a little, as though he were tired of holding up a smile.

"I'll catch up," Bailey insisted.

With no response, Rob shook his head and walked up the trail. Jude followed, but made a point to fix her eyes on Bailey. She squinted as if she could burn through the dense tension in the air. She paused and smiled crookedly before turning to playfully scamper up the trail.

"Horse face," Bailey muttered.

Bailey wandered around a fallen tree, feigning to look for the right spot to squat, when a wad of navy-blue cloth caught her attention. She reached down to pinch the rubberized fabric. A raincoat.

She yanked it up and held it out with both hands, examining the details. The color, the logo—even the little hole in the sleeve from a burning ember from last summer. She felt certain—*beyond* certain—that this was Rob's jacket. The possible explanations swirled in her head, but nothing could contest the fact that Rob had traveled up this trail before.

Bailey's eyes began to fill with tears. She wiped her sleeve across her face, took a few deep breaths, and walked back toward the trail, rain jacket in hand. The familiar smell of rain laced the breeze, and thunder rolled in the distance.

When the trail leveled out, Bailey looked out over the darkening valley—tall, white trees punctuated the blackening forest. The sounds of rushing water droned on from below.

Rob had already hung Jude's hammock and was starting on his own while Jude lounged and gawked at the fading sunset.

"Looks like it's your lucky day," Bailey said as he dropped the blue rain jacket at Rob's feet.

He closed his eyes for a moment, then looked back at Bailey. For the first time on the trip, he seemed to drop whatever act he had put on.

"I'm so sorry, Bailey."

Bailey had been ready to fire back with a bitter response, but his sincerity caught her off guard. She thought he might cry. Composing herself, she went for a softer approach.

"I just don't understand, Rob. I thought we were better friends than this," she said. "You lied to me."

He nodded. "I'm sorry."

Bailey sighed and glanced over her shoulder at Jude, who was busy digging through her pack.

"I don't understand what you see in her," Bailey said. "Where did she even come from? Is this a rebound thing or—"

"It's complicated." Rob shook his head. "But you and me... we are still friends... I love you, Bailey. I just need you to be patient—just for this trip."

Bailey folded her arms and waited for a little more explanation, but Rob's plain face made it clear—he had nothing else to offer.

"Alright," Bailey said.

"Thank you," he said in a thin breath, then went right back to setting up camp.

Dinner went on as expected. It might have been silent if not for Jude's pointless yet consistent blathering. When the rain began to fall, Bailey welcomed the end of the day and climbed into her hammock to sleep. The patter of light raindrops spotting the tarp above her soothed her to sleep.

It's hard to know how long she had slept before the howls outside grew too loud to ignore.

Bailey knew the sound of dogs, and she knew the sound of wolves. As she slowly accepted consciousness, the howls turned into whooping and grunting. She imagined what kind of animal could make such a sound. The hair on her neck stiffened.

Slowly, she rolled in her hammock to peek into the darkness, toward the quickening sounds.

Moonlight illuminated the gaunt aspen trees. She strained to see something in the darkness, but nothing moved. The hooting persisted, then multiplied. Three, four, maybe five voices rang out in a dissonant chorus.

A conversation began.

High-pitched tones dropped into a deep, guttural language. The unseen creatures seemed to speak back and forth in an inhuman dialect she couldn't recognize. The deep, gurgling vowels joined sharp hisses and hard vocal cracks—all to carry on a cryptic discussion. The dialogue grew louder, closer, and somehow smacked of profanity.

Bailey blinked away the sleep and focused on a tree that seemed to move in the breeze. A pale and impossibly tall figure stepped out from behind the tree. Stark-white skin reflected the moonlight. It was almost completely naked, except for a tattered, white fabric wrapped between its legs. Long strands of tangled hair covered its head and flowed down its body like greasy, pale vines. It looked so much like a wild man, except for its incredible height and emaciated frame. It turned and lifted its face upward, revealing its big, grinning maw. The smiling stupor turned into a howl that seemed to penetrate deep into the night air until other voices answered back.

Bailey's mouth went dry.

The creature walked in big strides. Its bony knees jutted out as it carefully chose its footing. It walked silently, spider-like, except for its ongoing gargling monologue.

A strong hand grabbed Bailey's shoulder from behind.

She jolted in terror, but another hand pressed up against her mouth to unsuccessfully stifle her scream.

Bailey felt relieved to see that the hands belonged to Rob. Still holding her tightly, he leaned his head over hers and whispered into her ear, "Trust me, it's better if you don't run."

She pushed his hand away from her mouth and forced out a sharp whisper, "What?!"

Bailey sat up and pushed Rob. He grabbed her wrist. "Shh…" He begged, but she squirmed, turned, and fell out of the hammock onto the soft forest ground. As she fell, her elbow jammed against a root, and she gasped.

Rob bent down and reached out for her, but he stopped as the strange, deep voices called out in a harsh staccato of foreign words. Then it spoke in garbled English.

"The agreement."

Bailey jerked her head back to look at the woods. Two other creatures came out of the forest to join the first. They all looked in her direction, and the first started off toward her with a massive stride as it called out.

"One dead or two living. No more settling for one, my dears; this time we take two living."

With a jolt, Bailey sprang to her bare feet and started sprinting back toward the trail.

"No! Bailey!" Rob shouted, but the whoops and hollers of the creatures drowned him out.

Bailey's feet slapped against the rocks and slid on loose earth as she sprinted deep into the darkness. The trail had become just a suggestion as she ran wildly away from the sickening sound. When her shin caught a stray tree root, she fell again on her swelling elbow.

She writhed and rolled onto her back, looking to see if they had chased after her.

Only the forest looked back.

She sat up and tried to catch her breath. The back of her throat throbbed. She coughed. The darkness seemed to thicken as she strained her eyes to see farther. The strange voices still murmured in the distance.

Long, ghastly clouds began to stretch across the moon, choking out the remaining light.

A twig snapped.

Bailey held her breath. She thought she heard footsteps but couldn't be sure over the sound of her pounding heartbeat.

A woman's voice said, "Bailey?"

The silhouette of a woman's head broke through from the edge of the darkness and into the faint remains of starlight. Jude. She hunched over and scurried through a patch of brush just past the little spot of ground Bailey had fallen into.

"Bailey," Jude called out in a shaking whisper.

"Jude," Bailey whispered hoarsely.

The two scrambled to find each other, and, as though by instinct, they clasped shivering hands.

"We've got to get out of here," Bailey started. "I don't know what's going on or what those things are, but Rob... We just need to go."

A bright, blue light shone above the edge of the trail. It was illuminated from one source, something long and oval in shape. It seemed to float three feet above the ground. It slowly and silently cruised between trees.

Bailey choked on her saliva as pulsating, humming sounds swelled from the approaching light.

Jude pressed her body against Bailey. "Don't be afraid."

Bailey slowly turned her gaze away from the floating light and instead toward the stoic face of Jude. The blue light cast an eerie hue across Jude's rigid face, highlighting her pronounced cheekbones and deep-set eyes. Her skin began to stretch, deepening her eye sockets and baring her teeth.

"My family wants to meet you," Jude said.

Bailey fell back and scrambled away until a large rock stopped her progress. She sucked in deep breaths and broke into a sudden sweat.

Jude stood upright. Her legs and arms grew to an unnatural length, and her flowing hair draped downward across her body. Her eyes looked like dark pools of oil, with just a fraction of blue light shining back.

"Don't be afraid." Jude's voice dropped into a low, guttural tone. "We have an agreement we have never broken and never will."

Bailey struggled to her feet.

Jude opened her mouth to reveal a wet, frostbitten tongue. "One dead or two living. We'd rather have two living."

Run.

Tree branches lashed at Bailey's arms and face as she sprinted deeper into the woods. She followed her shadow, cast in a sickening blue light that intensified all around her.

She lunged ahead, but the ground had turned downward, and she tumbled over a stretch of thick foliage and down into a wet ravine. Hitting the ground knocked out her breath, but she sprang back up to her hands and scrambled on.

A haggard, gargled scream echoed from behind. Still running, Bailey jerked around to see what had made the horrid sound.

The creature, whom she knew as Jude, was joined by three others. The four tall, white freaks closed in on her like it took no effort at all. One, a male, reached out with a gnarled hand. The fingernails were chipped and packed with soil.

"Lucky hour! Two living!" It squealed.

Bailey juked to the left. She glanced to find a new route when she was confronted with an object. Soon after she collided with the obstacle, it let out a terrified scream. A deer. Only a young deer. She crashed to the ground yet again, and shame washed over her briefly as the animal crumbled and wailed.

As she struggled to gain control of her trembling legs, a knotted, pale hand grabbed her throat.

Bailey gasped.

Face-to-face with its blonde, sunken face, she slapped and scratched, but it just stared into her. It looked through her eyes, past her skull, and into her head.

"Let go!" Bailey screamed.

It lifted her by the neck, high into the air. Tilting its head to one side, then the other, it looked her over with its deep-set black eyes. The smell of filthy hair filled each labored gasp for air.

With a flick of its finger, it beckoned the other creatures over to take a look. Jude stood back, looking pleased with herself.

The quietest of the four leaned in close. It closed one eye and craned its face in toward Bailey's.

"Shh," it hissed, then jammed two fingers into her mouth as if to count her teeth.

Bailey gagged and kicked at the creatures, but they hardly seemed to notice.

The woods went silent, except for the injured deer that screeched and rocked on the ground. The creatures slowed their movement and settled into a stoic calm, only swelling with each inhale through their open jaws.

A blue glow filled the spaces between the trees. It thickened and seemed to turn into a heavy bioluminescence—a living fog that sought to fill every void. A hum, then a pulse, and finally a massive, floating vessel appeared a few yards away. It was silver but showed no reflection. No doors could be seen or any notable features—just a long, missile-like craft. While it wasn't much taller than the 10-foot-tall creatures, the strange craft stretched long into the woods like an immense, silver cigar.

A spiral of light appeared on the outer wall of the craft, twisting into an open porthole.

The deer's cries carried on in a relentless, dissonant song.

"Two living," the creature grunted and threw Bailey, head-first into the gaping hull of the strange ship.

She curled into a fetal ball, shielding her face. The ground felt hard and smooth.

"Bailey," Rob called from across the room.

She hesitated to look, hoping it was all a nightmare.

"I…" Rob's words trembled, "I'm sorry. I didn't want to die."

Bailey peeked out at the pewter-colored walls surrounding her. Everything looked smooth, curved, and plain. Across the room, the floor dropped downward as if a whirlpool had been frozen into the stone floor. Trapped, Rob stretched out his fingertips from the center.

"I wanted to surprise you," Rob said. "I came to scope out the trail alone. I wanted to bring you, Bailey. I did, but what I saw was... the *Nordics*—or that's what they call themselves. They had come from... I don't know, but they aren't from Earth."

Bailey crept closer to the hole in the floor, getting a better view. Rob stood uncomfortably in the center of a deep, concave cone. Gravity pushed him downward, and he struggled to find a way to stand. He wiped his face on his sleeve.

"They said they have an agreement with mankind—once a year, in these woods, *one dead or two living.*"

He sniffed and pressed his lips together.

"They were going to kill me, Bailey." He said. "One dead… They'd bring me back, dead, to wherever they came from... unless I…"

Bailey's mouth dropped. "Rob, what did you do?"

"I'm sorry about the way things went, but..." Rob tried to climb up the side of the slippery cone, gritting his teeth. "When I was sure they would kill me, all I could think about was you, Bailey. They gave me a choice and made Jude come along with me to make sure you..."

Bailey sighed. "Two living."

Rob raked his hands through his hair and choked down his tears.

With a sigh, Bailey rolled over to her back and hid her face with her hands. The muffled cries of the deer rang through the awkward silence.

"Do you hate me?" Rob pleaded.

The crying from outside grated on Bailey's ears. She rubbed her temples in long, slow circles.

"Bailey?"

"Bailey?"

Silence won as the deer made its final cry.

A sharp crack startled Bailey and Rob.

The spiral portal opened up into a tall doorway.

One creature leaned into the opening and snarled, baring its teeth and drooling. It twisted its long torso and flung the body of the dead deer onto the cold floor with a sickening thud.

"One dead!"

The slobbering creature lunged forward, snarling and pointing its jagged finger at Bailey. Huffing and spitting, it lashed out in a furious tantrum but would not touch Bailey—like it was suddenly forbidden to lay a finger on her.

"One dead," it snorted. "The agreement is met!"

A bluish smoke fell from the ceiling. As it reached Bailey, she found it hard to keep her eyes open. The symphony of mourning creatures faded to the background as she succumbed to sleep.

In a blur of dreamed or imagined wind, Bailey drifted into nothingness. For the first time in a long time, she didn't care about anything—not Rob or the Nordics. She left no care for her own well-being. If the next breath never came, all would be just as well.

Nothing.

Birds chirped. The warmth of the sun and the tickle of a fresh breeze woke her.

Bailey opened her eyes.

The daylight welcomed her back to the woods. Several minutes passed before she gained enough strength to sit.

When she forced herself up, there Rob was.

They looked at each other, sitting in stony silence, remembering everything and still not saying a word.

Two living.

MADICUL ISLAND
BY SCOTT SEPPI

Valparaiso, Chile. A rusty steamer sat in port. Its trip around the horn had been rough, and there had been extensive damage. At the harbor bar sat the expedition's sponsor, a small, squirrely man with a quick mind and an even quicker mouth. He pondered ways to fund the repairs while his tea grew cold. The captain sat next to him and drank beer as fast as they could bring it to him. The storm hadn't just wrecked his ship, but his nerves as well.

The passengers were a desperate group of men. Hard-luck losers who'd been dealt a rotten hand or had squandered the hand they'd once held. They were bound for Alaska and the great gold rush. Much of their gear had been lost, swept overboard in the heavy seas. Those with cash scoured the nearby shops to re-equip. Those who hadn't were left to their own devices. They'd already begged, borrowed, stolen, and more to get this far. There wasn't much they wouldn't do.

It wasn't long before the Valparaiso residents were anxious for them to leave. The passengers themselves were just as anxious. It was already late in the year. They'd be frozen out of the northern ports if they didn't get underway soon.

The mining gear wasn't all that had washed off the decks. Half the ship's liquor was lost as well. One of the miners had grown up bootlegging and knew an opportunity when he saw it. These men were a thirsty bunch. When the liquor ran out, whatever he could brew, ferment, or distill would be in high demand. A quart for a hammer, two for a pick, and a few gallons would have him better equipped than before.

As the others scrounged for mining supplies, he sought out a still. He could afford the rig, but he couldn't afford to feed it. The storekeeper, sensing a lost sale, told him of a valley filled with berries. Nobody bothered them because they were at the end of a mile-long, brush-choked trail. A free machete and a burlap sack to help close the sale were more than the desperate man could resist.

It took him half a day to hack his way through the dense, woody growth that covered the abandoned trail before he came upon the valley. In the midst of a sea of tall grass was an enormous bush covered in blackberries. The largest he'd ever seen. His feet crunched over what sounded like dry branches that were hidden in the grass. In front of the bush stood a signpost; its faded sign was bleached white, its message lost to time and the sun's rays.

It didn't take long for him to collect enough berries to make gallons of liquor—more than enough. When his sack was full, he set it down and began to eat the berries straight from the thorny vines. He needed to build his strength before hauling the heavy load up the trail.

It wasn't until he was nearly full that he saw a tiny worm squirm out from within one of the berry's nodules. He squashed a nodule from another berry and looked through the pulp. There was another worm. He tried nodule after nodule from berry after berry and found a worm in each. It gave him a sick feeling for a moment. He reminded himself that he'd once picked maggots out of meat to avoid starvation. A nearly microscopic worm was nothing. Even so, it killed his appetite. He hefted the sack over his shoulder and returned to the docks.

He made it back to the steamer as they were undergoing final preparations to leave port. The captain wasn't happy with the repairs and doubted they would reach their final destination. While the captain was correct that they wouldn't make an Alaskan port, he could never have predicted the reason why.

The five friends, Betty, Eddie, Ron, Jim, and Stacy, stood on the rocky beach at dawn. Together, they made up the entire class of 1957, the largest ever for the small Alaskan town.

"The beach!" scoffed Stacy. "This is where we're having our senior sendoff?"

She was a tall blonde girl who looked like she belonged on the cover of a magazine. She was the best-looking girl for a hundred miles in any direction. "I swear, Betty. I thought even a Suzie homemaker like you had more sense than this."

"What's wrong with the beach?" Betty asked, sounding hurt.

Stacy rolled her eyes and let out an exaggerated sigh. "What's wrong?" laughed Stacy. "If this were a California beach, or a Hawaiian beach, or any other beach with sand and sun, then it would've been a great idea. I don't know if you've noticed, but the water is freezing and the shore is nothing but rocks and seaweed. I can't even sit anywhere without getting my pants wet!"

"At least something gets your pants wet," joked Jim, a tall young man who would've been as attractive as Stacy were it not for his overly large, overly square forehead.

"Come on, you two. Don't get started," said Eddie, Betty's longtime boyfriend.

"Don't mind Jim," replied Stacy dismissively. "He's been mad ever since he found out that being prom king and queen together didn't mean we were required by law to go steady."

"Quit trying to make me sound stupid," Jim protested. "I was just seeing if you'd fall for it."

"So you think I'm dumb enough to believe—" began Stacy before she was abruptly cut off.

"This isn't going to be a beach party," interrupted Ron. "It's going to be an island party," he said, pointing to the fog-shrouded island that lay just beyond the shore.

"And how are we supposed to get there?" asked Stacy incredulously. "We can't take a boat. The whole island is ringed with jagged rocks hiding just below the surface. Everyone knows that."

"We're going to walk," replied Ron.

"And you all think I'm the stupid one," laughed Jim.

"We're going to have a century tide today and tomorrow," said Ron impatiently. "According to my dad, the water will go so low that the island will become a peninsula, and we can simply walk across the rocks."

"Okay, whatever you guys," snapped Stacy. "You can't seriously expect me to go. Give me one good reason why I'd want to climb a bunch of slimy wet rocks to go to a stupid island with nothing on it."

"Because it's an adventure!" pleaded Betty. "It's something we'll remember forever, and if you think about it, this might be the last thing we all do together. You're going to college in Arizona; Ron is going to the Air Force; Eddie is joining up with the Coast Guard; and Jim's probably going to be dead in five years at the hands of a jealous husband."

"Hey!" shouted Jim.

"I'm going to miss you too," said Stacy. "But why would we have to go to the island to have this last memory of us together?"

"I'll give you twenty-two and a half reasons," said Betty as Eddie removed and opened his backpack. "Eighteen bottles of beer, three bottles of wine, half a bottle of bourbon, and nobody to bother us for twelve hours while the tide is in."

"Alright, you chickens, what are you waiting for?" commanded Stacy.

As the tide receded, the five friends began their journey across the newly exposed peninsula. It was roughly fifty yards to the island, but thanks to the seaweed-slicked rocks, the going was slow. Only the barnacles kept them from sliding into the cold Alaskan waters.

"This is going to be, like, crazy cool!" exclaimed Ron. "We'll be the first people on Madigul Island in nearly a hundred years, maybe even the first people ever!"

"Not the first ever; there was the gold rush shipwreck," said Eddie.

"The gold rush shipwreck?" asked Ron.

"Yeah, my grandfather told me about it when I was little," Eddie replied. "Back during the gold rush, a Louisiana schooner had sailed around Cape Horn at the wrong time of year and got beat up pretty badly. It ran aground on the rocks on the back side of the island. Some of them made it to the island. Only one of them made it to the main shore, where my Gramps found him.

Gramps brought him to what passed for a hospital back then and sat with him. The man woke long enough to tell his story before getting violently ill and finally slipping into a coma. Gramps was sure the man was going to die, but later that night, the man bolted upright and attacked him. He bit into his face and ruined his eye. He said the man acted crazy, possessed, and was yelling about how hungry he was. Three men couldn't pull him off my Gramps. The doc had to do it with a shotgun round to the head. They say his arms and legs flailed for hours afterwards. That's how my Gramps, Gunnlaugur Johnson, earned the nickname 'One-eyed Johnson'."

"That's pretty weird," said Jim.

"That's not the weird part," replied Eddie. "The weird part is that when they managed to get a rescue boat to the island, everybody was dead; it looked like they had killed each other and torn each other apart.

They buried all the pieces they could find, and nobody has come back since. The following summer, the birds that used to live on the island went crazy and went to war with each other. Within a week, there were no more birds on the island. That's how it got the name Mad Gull Island."

"I thought it was named Madigul Island," said Betty.

"Gramps had such a thick accent that Madigul is how everyone heard it," said Eddie. "It doesn't actually have an official name. On the map, it's just a number. There are more islands up here than people to name them."

"And this is the place we're going to spend the day drinking?" asked Jim. "Creepy."

"But memorable," replied Eddie.

"How much of that is true?" Ron asked.

"I'm pretty sure the shipwreck happened," said Eddie. "Other people have told stories about it, but none as colorful as the one Gramps told. Is it true though? Well, all I can say is that Gramps told a lot of stories while he was alive."

Together, they climbed the last few yards of rock. Ron shot ahead of everyone else and took his first step onto the island.

"First!" he yelled, and then laughed a taunting laugh.

"First on the island and last in looks," replied Jim.

"Come on, you guys, hurry up," said Jim as he joined Ron on the island. "We're wasting good drinking time."

The five friends walked through a strand of evergreens, stunted and twisted from strong winds and short summers. They emerged into a large meadow that was covered in shin-high grass that was dotted with low shrubs and ferns. In the middle of the meadow was an enormous thicket of blackberry vines that twisted and piled over twelve feet high.

As they crossed the meadow, their steps were noisy with the sound of twigs and small branches crunching beneath their feet.

"Holy moly, would you look at all these berries? I've never seen such huge blackberry bushes. Look at the size of these canes; they're as thick as tree branches, and these berries are gigantic!" exclaimed Stacy excitedly.

"That's one of the benefits of there not being any birds around to eat them. I bet in fifty years this whole island is going to be one giant blackberry bush," said Ron.

Ron and Jim joined Stacy and began gorging on blackberries, while Eddie and Betty wandered to the opposite side of the thicket. The grass brushed past their legs, and the twigs and branches crunched underneath. When out of sight, Eddie took Betty by the arms and pulled her close. They kissed gently at first, quickly growing more passionate and aggressive.

Betty dropped to her knees, pulling Eddie down with her. She lay on her back and cried out in pain. She went to move the branches that had poked her and pulled from a tangle of grass a handful of small, sharp bones.

She gasped and jumped to her feet, showing the bones to Eddie. He felt along the ground and picked up his own handful of them. "Holy cow, Gramps was right. These are bird bones. Look at all of these!" he exclaimed as he pulled handful after handful from below the grass.

They ran to the other side of the thicket to show the others. Ron and Jim each held a beer, and Stacy was drinking wine straight from the bottle. Their mouths were ringed in purple blackberry juice.

"And what were you two lovebirds doing?" asked Jim in a teasing tone.

"Finding this," answered Betty, handing him the bones.

"Cool bones, so what?" Jim asked.

"It's not the bones," said Eddie. "It's how many of them there are. This whole field is covered in them!"

The boys began walking around the blackberry bush, searching with their feet. They had a hard time finding a plot of ground that wasn't blanketed with bones. Stacy stood next to Betty and watched as the boys wandered all throughout the large meadow. Bones crunched beneath their feet wherever they walked.

Stacy's face had grown pale. She dropped the wine bottle and held her stomach tightly.

"You know what, guys? I'm leaving. I'm not spending all day in a bird graveyard," she said flatly, and she walked as quickly as she could through the meadow and towards the shore. The rest of the group followed close behind, with Jim calling for her to wait up.

When she reached the end of the island, she began climbing across the rocky peninsula. Jim followed closely behind. Ron turned to look at Eddie and Betty, neither appeared to be interested in leaving. "Aren't you coming?" Ron asked.

"I think we'll stay and, uh, explore the island," said Betty.

"Explore, I see," Ron said, smiling. He then turned to follow Jim and Stacy to the mainland shore.

"Our private island paradise—what could be more romantic?" asked Betty with a laugh.

"Indeed," Eddie replied as suavely as he could. He put his arms around her, and they began kissing.

"Hubba-hubba!" yelled Jim from the shore.

"Come on," said Eddie, let's get the backpack and get out of sight of these jokers."

They walked back through the trees and into the meadow. Eddie retrieved the backpack and counted the remaining liquor. He let out a sigh of relief that plenty remained. Betty began eating the berries from the sprawling thicket.

"Let's go," said Eddie.

"Go where?"

"You know, go find a place to pick up where we left off."

She smiled at him coyly. "Give me some time to get back in the mood. This is a pretty creepy place."

"It's not too creepy to pig out on berries," he said impatiently.

"Come on, don't be mean. Try some of these; they're delicious."

"I can't touch 'em. I'm allergic. My skin gets covered in hives. Too many, and my throat will swell shut."

"I'm sorry, I didn't know. Let's go," she said as she picked a small handful and began walking. "I should really know these things about my future husband," she said energetically.

"Don't be a spaz," he joked.

They walked across the meadow towards the back side of the island. They weaved through a sparse strand of madrona trees with their twisted trunks and orange-peeled skin. At the end of the island was a bare, rocky plateau that abutted the sea. It had been worn smooth from the fall rains and the winter tides.

The summer sun was warm. They stood and held hands as they looked out over the open water as it disappeared over the horizon. The water below was littered with rocks. Some stood proud of the water, and many lay just below the surface. "Do you think this is where the ship wrecked?" asked Betty. "It must've been terrible out in that water," she continued, not waiting for an answer.

"Probably," replied Eddie, growing annoyed that she seemed to be completely out of the mood.

"Where do you think they buried, you know..." She paused. "The pieces of the survivors?"

"Couldn't tell you," he said as he sat on a flat stone that was warm from the sun.

She sat next to him and laid her head on his lap. He ran his fingers through her hair. She had already decided to let him go all the way and had drunk steadily during the walk to get over her nerves. Between the liquor, the warm sun, and his hand gently caressing her, she fell asleep.

When he heard the first of her snores, he looked up to the sky and stifled a frustrated scream. After a dozen minutes of deep breaths, the painful swelling in his pants receded. Not long afterwards, he too fell asleep.

She woke with a start to the sound of snoring. Eddie was lying flat on the rock. The backpack was under his head, and her head had been on his chest. As she sat up, he began to wake. When he saw the sun heading low on the horizon, he leapt to his feet and looked at his watch before first letting out a sigh of relief and then a grunt of frustration at how much time they had wasted sleeping.

He sat back down next to her. They looked out over the water in silence. Eddie looked at his watch again.

"I figure we've got less than an hour left before we have to head back, or we'll lose the tide and have to spend the night here. Personally, I wouldn't mind staying, but I think by morning your parents would be waiting on the shore to kill us both."

"Then maybe we should make good use of the time," she said awkwardly, turning to him.

"Whoa!" he exclaimed. "Would you look at your lips?"

"Oh my God, what's wrong with them?"

"It's the berries," he laughed. "You remember the way your grandma used to wear her lipstick?"

"Oh no!" she gasped.

"Oh yes!" he laughed again. "Here, let me clean them off."

"What, you don't want to taste my berry-sweet lips?"

"That was pretty bad," he groaned. "I just don't want my lips to swell up and itch," he replied. He took the Bourbon from his backpack and wet his kerchief with it. He dabbed the berry juice off her lips and then began to kiss her. He lay against the large, smooth rock and pulled her on top of him. They kissed deeply and passionately. His one hand held the back of her head, his fingers tangled in her hair. With his other hand, he first unbuttoned his pants, then ran his hand up and under the back of her shirt, then slowly back down and under the back of her pants, waiting for resistance but getting none.

He grabbed her by the cheek and pressed her tightly against his pelvis. Her eyes shot open, and she violently pushed him away. She jumped to her feet, kneeing him in the groin in the process. She ran to the strand of madrona trees and began to vomit violently.

When she stopped retching, she moaned in pain. "I need to go home!" she yelled while holding her stomach. She ran through the trees and into the meadow.

Eddie gripped his crotch with both hands and fought his own urge to vomit from the pain of his traumatized testicles. By the time he managed to stand and button his pants, she was already across the island.

He ran with an ungainly gallop as the pain in his groin raged. As he ran through the meadow and past the blackberry thicket, his foot caught under a vine hidden by the grass and fell forward, the massive thorns from the vine piercing the skin on his arms.

From the ground, he could see a hollowed-out space in the center of the thicket. Inside, he saw the massive, ancient canes from which the rest of the thicket had grown. They were the size of small tree trunks.

He got up slowly and carefully, pulling the thorns from his arms. He heard Betty scream a horrified, blood-curdling scream in the distance. He stood and ran towards the screams. If she'd fallen into the water, he wouldn't have long to get to her before the currents took her out to sea.

When he got to the end of the island, he stopped cold and fought his own urge to scream.

Eddie looked out onto the mainland beach and watched in horror as Stacy knelt over Betty's body. Her face was covered in blood, and she made primitive guttural sounds as she hungrily fed on Betty's corpse.

"Stacy, stop!" Eddie yelled. He wanted to run and stop her by himself, but fear held him frozen in shock. His brain struggled to comprehend what he was seeing.

"I'm sorry, Eddie. I'm just so hungry, so damned hungry!" Stacy shouted back. Her words came out in tortured screeches. She stood up from her meal and cast a fixed stare at Eddie. "I'm so damned hungry, Eddie! Maybe you can help me not be hungry anymore! Why don't you come help me, Eddie? You're my pal, right?"

Stacy stood tall, then hunched over with a jolt as though she'd been punched in the gut. She tightly gripped her abdomen with one hand and walked unsteadily towards the peninsula, stopping after a few steps to look back at Betty's corpse as though she were deciding if it were safe to leave her meal unattended.

"What the hell is wrong with you, Stacy?" Eddie screamed. He saw the twisted, horrific look on Stacy's face, as though her body and mind were wracked with intractable pain. Her eyes were wide, and the whites had turned blood red. Fear made him abandon any thought of comforting her.

"I'm hungry, Eddie! Can't you help me? So very, very hungry!" she screeched. "Why don't you come here so I don't have to come to you? No? Okay, Eddie, I just thought you'd be a pal. Maybe we could be more than pals? We could kiss the way you and Betty used to kiss. Will you come kiss me? No?" She screeched as she began walking towards him again. "You know you'll never kiss anyone prettier than me!"

She began climbing the peninsula's rocks. The water had begun reaching its top as the tide came in. Even though the waves were soaking her, she persisted in moving forward despite having trouble keeping her balance. "So hungry, Eddie, why won't you help me?"

Eddie searched the ground for a weapon, some way to defend himself. He took a handful of rocks and began throwing them at Stacy in a desperate bid to stop her from reaching the island. She was only a few yards away when a lucky throw hit her in the head hard enough to cause her to stumble. A wave crested over the rocks and pulled her into the water. She let out an inhuman scream and thrashed wildly. She couldn't keep her head above the water, and she soon drowned. The current pulled her lifeless body out to sea.

He stared helplessly at Betty's body as it lay crumpled on the rocky shore. Even if he were able to reach her, he knew there was nothing he could do.

He sat and cried until he began to grow numb. Now stranded, he began yelling for help until his throat grew sore. He sat on the rocks and lit a cigarette, then scratched at his arms where the blackberry thorns had caught him. A nasty case of hives was beginning to form. He felt a twinge in his lungs. His asthma would be a problem soon. Had he been clear-headed, he'd have considered taking the risk and crossing the peninsula before the tide fully came in, but his mind was overcome by what he'd just witnessed.

He took drag after drag off the cigarette, trying to make sense of what had happened. He began to drink, trying to keep hold of his sanity and put a stop to the visions of the carnage at the beach.

He wasn't sure what had startled him awake, but it took several moments to gain his bearings. The sun had disappeared below the horizon, and the moon was well into its journey across the sky. It cast a pale blue light over the island and the shore, turning the blood that covered Betty's corpse black.

The hives on his arms had grown worse, and the itch was unbearable. He had to work to breathe. He cupped the lighter's flame and lit a fresh cigarette. Over the sound of the wind and the surf, he again heard the commotion that had woken him. He looked up to see an explosion of sparks over an orange glow that filtered through the tree line. The town was burning.

Over the sparks and distant roar of the fire, he heard muted screams. One scream sounded louder and closer. It was filled with terror. He looked down from the tree line and towards the shore, where he saw an older woman stumble and run from out of the woods. When the moonlight caught her face, he recognized her as Mrs. Jorgenson, the school principal. Behind her, he saw Ron running hard while holding his side.

"Why won't you help me, Mrs. Jorgenson!" he shouted through strained vocal chords. "I'm just so hungry, so damned hungry!"

She stumbled and fell, and Ron pounced, landing on her back and pinning her down. He chewed through the back of her neck until her struggling and screaming came to an abrupt halt.

Eddie quickly snuffed his cigarette and quietly backed into the strand of trees, not wanting to be seen. He stood behind a tree and peered through the branches.

Ron continued to feast on his former principal's corpse, hungrily devouring her innards, tearing the muscle from her bones. He began vomiting violently, retching until he was empty. "So damned hungry!" he cried to the sky in frustration, and then began to feed again. Eddie had to get away from the sound before he lost his mind. He quietly walked back to the meadow and opened his backpack. He needed the Bourbon and he needed another cigarette.

First Stacy, now Ron, he thought to himself. *What the hell is happening? This can't be real!*

He looked at the massive thicket of blackberries. It had an otherworldly appearance in the moonlight and rippled in waves as the wind blew over and through it. The sight filled him with a deep fear. The sound of the leaves rustling in the wind seemed to speak to him. It made his hair stand on end. His entire body itched as though he were covered head to toe in hives.

He thought of the stories that Gramps used to tell him about this island, about the shipwreck, about the survivor who had taken his eye. It really was true, and Eddie felt—he knew—that the blackberries were the cause of it, and he thought he knew how.

He found a stick and wrapped his kerchief tightly around the end. He took a swig of Bourbon, then used the rest to soak the head of his makeshift torch. He walked to where he had tripped earlier and squatted down to look more closely at the hollow in the thicket. That's when he saw that beside the largest, oldest cluster of canes was a flat stone. It was a grave marker. This was where they'd buried the shipwreck victims. The blackberry thicket had grown from seeds in the stomachs of the corpses. This was the source of the evil plague. He set the thicket alight and stepped back to watch it burn.

Eddie watched as the fire engulfed the blackberry thicket. The flames climbed high into the sky, and the fire crackled loudly. He backed into the strand of trees as the meadow caught fire.

"Eddie! I know you're over there," Ron's voice screeched on the wind. "Come on, Eddie, I need your help; I'm so hungry! The principal tried to help; she always tried to help. But she couldn't help me, Eddie. I'm still so hungry!" Eddie stood and lit his last cigarette. Ron continued calling to him, screech-pleading for help. Eddie stayed in the trees, looking out onto the shore with the fire from the blackberry bush raging behind him. He scratched at his arm while watching Ron continue to eat the principal with such vigor that he broke his teeth on her bones.

As dawn approached, he heard the ring of the city fire bell. The volunteer fire brigade had finally made it to town. Shortly afterwards, he heard a gunshot, and then another. He ran to the edge of the island and looked at the mainland. In the early morning light, he saw a figure run from the forest and onto the shore. It was Jim, hunched over and running as fast as he could, screeching incoherently. A group of figures burst from the forest. They fired at him as he ran across the open rocks. The bullets hit their mark, and Jim went stiff, falling face first, his body twitching wildly.

"Help me, Eddie!" Ron screeched and ran to the rocky peninsula. He climbed desperately through the water, bracing himself on the rocks that had just begun to break the surface of the receding tide. The men's rifles knocked him into the sea. His lifeless body was carried away by the current.

Eddie began to shake. He fell to his knees and began to cry in relief that his nightmare was nearly over.

The men circled Jim's body and were beating him in the head with the butt of their guns, trying to stop him from thrashing. The man who appeared to be in charge of the group walked to the peninsula and watched Ron's body as it was being carried away by the current. He watched where it was heading so he could retrieve it once they were finished dealing with the bodies on the beach.

The man in charge looked over to see Eddie shaking, crying, and clawing at his hive covered arm. "You there, hey, are you alright? Do you need help!" he shouted.

"Yes!" Eddie shouted. "I need help; please, help me!"

The man started climbing the rocks and surveyed the situation. It wouldn't be long before the tide had receded enough to cross.

"Alright, kid, it looks like I'll be able to get there soon. You're going to be alright, okay?"

"Just please hurry," Eddie said frantically, the pitch of his voice rising to a screech. "I'm just so hungry, so damned hungry!"

THE KILL

BY QUIET RED

The world has a looming darkness soaked deep into its marrow. This darkness is so profoundly lurid that its mere presence can blacken the Earth's flora. When the shadows turn and bare their crooked teeth, the SRA moves to intercept it. The Supernatural Regulation Agency (SRA) is a government-backed organization positioned as humankind's first line of defense for this darkness. Emerging in the late 1950s and consisting of former special forces soldiers who engaged in unsanctioned vigilantism against the supernatural, the organization garnered worldwide attention from the effective tactics they employed and the undeniable results that followed. The organization was officially sanctioned by the United Nations in the 1960s and given full international agency. The SRA now enforces humanity's official regulation and policing of the supernatural. Headquartered in the paranormal lightning rod of a city known as Redding Hollow, Connecticut, the SRA operates missions across the globe to protect human lives from the things that dare to make a peep in the night.

The current commander of the SRA, Commander Vernon Balecrest, is a man with copious amounts of baggage to lug into battle against the darkness. He's experienced heavy personal loss by its tenebrous hands—the hands of a dark spirit. Balecrest's life had been utterly torn apart when he came home to find his adoring wife covered in the blood of his two young children. Delilah, his beautiful muse, his everything, was sitting on the floor among their wound-riddled bodies, drawing pictures with their entrails and mumbling to herself. She seemed to be completely incognizant of her actions. Though it wasn't truly her behind the eyes. It was pure evil—an evil that Balecrest vowed to stamp out. Ignorant of a less fatal way to stop a possession victim, Balecrest lost his wife on that dark evening as well. This loss was the catalyst to his incursion of the darkness.

The one thing Balecrest desires more than anything else is the capture and identification of this spirit and all those like it. The phenomenon is rare, but not unheard of. Unfortunately, each time the SRA gets close to one, it somehow escapes their grasp. Of the countless supernatural occurrences that plague humankind, that of a dark spirit possession is most contentious for Balecrest, which is what makes the analyst's findings particularly energizing. SRA analysts scour the globe and decipher all information and findings the SRA acquires, looking for instances requiring the interference of the organization. The slender, bifocal wearing man heads into the bullpen where Balecrest is mulling around. The man is almost tripping over his own feet with nervous energy.

"Sir. We've received a report I think you'll be interested in. We have info on an active serial killer."

"A serial ki—that's a job for local police," Balecrest responds, with a shake of his head and a dismissive wave of the hand.

"Sir, we believe this one is a possession."

The SRA commander immediately drops his hands and shifts his tone. His eyes squint and his jaw clenches. "You're kidding… Where?"

"Mississippi, sir."

Before the analyst can even respond, Balecrest waves his arm in the air in a circular motion above his head, "We've got a live one! Everybody who isn't attached to a case, get eyes on this now." Balecrest turns to the analyst. "Get me a list of available Blue Coats."

Balecrest's immediate call for Blue Coats demands attention. SRA

Blue Coats are not unlike the overpowered US Marshalls of the SRA. They are highly trained and operate with relative impunity, so long as they get results. Any underworld fiend knows that if a Blue Coat is after you, you're either as good as dead or, if you're lucky, captured. They aren't sent for simple crowd control or policing. They're sent to wrap things up.

The killer has become infamous enough to earn a tabloid name: The Mississippi River Strangler. The name is indicative of the killer's modus operandi, one to strangle victims and dump their bodies in the Mississippi. The bodies, mostly vagabonds, were found in various locations after being dragged down river by the current, making it difficult for the police to pinpoint exactly where the killer is operating, not to mention the interference of nature itself. If this is indeed a dark spirit possession, the local police will be woefully ill-informed.

The bloodlust displayed by this killer can only be a bad thing. Although, unsure of its goal, the SRA believe that a dark spirit of this prolificacy will no doubt become a menace to the public at a disturbing level. Not only that, but whatever its motivations are must be like an evil clarion call. Dark spirits are driven by events from the life they lived before death. They are often anchored by hatred and other dark emotions, earthbound and unable to move on. From the looks of it, this spirit must have some serious pent-up rage.

The last dark spirit possession the SRA had dealt with was attempting to open a dimensional doorway to a hellish realm. In order to avoid something on that scale from happening, the Higher-Ups (unseen government shadow management at the SRA) are hellbent on getting this dealt with as soon as possible. The caveat is that Balecrest wants the spirit captured.

In touching base with their contact in Jacksonville, the SRA felt the killer most likely resides in Mississippi or Louisiana. The decision was made to move silently, in an effort not to spook the killer or risk the culprit catching wind of the operation, so Balecrest elects to send a Blue

Coat to pursue the case. In fact, in this instance, he opts to send two, and Balecrest has the perfect pair in mind for this case. Assigning two Blue Coats to a single case is an unusual practice, but in this instance, Balecrest sees a good reason for it. The killer is obviously dangerous, and with possession in the mix, the stakes are even higher.

Balecrest makes it clear that he wants the killer caught and captured. Not only that, but he's explicitly stated that the spirit be exorcised and contained, separate from the vessel. This calls for a special skill not every Blue Coat is equipped with. So, they recruit one of their best exorcists, an agent named Reed. A former priest, Reed is an excellent Blue Coat and highly capable; however, he's been known to be a bit too hesitant to take the fatal shot. Hence, why Balecrest wants to send a partner. For their second choice, they pick one of their loose cannons, agent Bourke. Bourke is a lauded agent with a prolific record, but he's also got one of the highest body counts among the Blue Coats. The Higher-Ups believe his reckless and trigger-happy nature will be balanced well against Reed's more patient and cautious approach. Conversely, they believe Bourke's propensity for a violent solution may keep Reed on his toes. On this particular assignment, the SRA doesn't want Bourke to end up just killing the Strangler, but they can't risk one of their best exorcists being killed for hesitating, either.

The two, particularly Bourke, aren't all that happy about the partnership. When they're brought in to be briefed, Bourke arrives first. As Reed approaches, he can hear his soon-to-be partner raising hell about the situation. The sentiment is mutual, but Reed walks in the briefing room, mid vitriol and unfazed. Ever the professional, Reed simply gives Bourke a sly wink and takes a seat, clearly infuriating the hotheaded Bourke, to Reed's amusement. Despite their mutual objection to the pairing, they are forced to take the assignment, anyway.

The reluctant duo is sent to meet with their contact in the Jackson police department, traveling by car, together. The contact, a local detective, has been keeping in touch with the SRA and running the investigation on the Strangler, from Jackson. Bourke and Reed are specifically instructed not to reveal themselves to the local PD or anyone else, only the contact. The two Blue Coats arrive in Jackson, staying at a hotel in the city while they're gathering info and collecting information from the detective. Getting to work immediately, the agents have the detective meet them at the hotel to consult, brainstorming ideas to plan their next steps.

On the agents' second night in Jackson, the police find another body, this time in Suspoena County. The body raises a few questions, as it's furthest north of any body found so far. The body was discovered by a civilian, caught up in an underwater thatch within the river. The body was untouched by animal life and showed minimal signs of struggle, aside from brutal strangulation. The trachea and esophagus were crushed, indicating either great leverage in the strangulation, or supernatural strength. At this point, the agents aren't sure which. In dealing with possessions, it could be either case, or even both. Regardless, the brutality of the killer is seen firsthand, and the minimal signs of struggle imply a killer who values the element of surprise.

Reed begins theorizing aloud as Bourke listens hesitantly. "I'm thinking the killer must've dumped the body around that area. It just hadn't been washed downstream quite as far since it got hung up in that thatch."

Unable to disagree with Reed, Bourke responds, "Whatever the case, the dumping grounds had to be north o' there."

"Yeah. Looks like we've got another road trip ahead of us." Bourke, not looking at Reed, stands with his arms crossed and grunts begrudgingly.

The Blue Coats travel an excruciatingly awkward hour and forty minutes to the small town of Brayerville, arriving mid-morning. The quaint location resides in Suspoena County, on the east bank of the Mississippi. The town is fairly barren. Calling it small is an understatement. The two find that there are no hotels or motels anywhere within the town, a fact that irritates Bourke in particular.

"Man, this place sucks. What the hell kind o' town doesn't even have a flophouse?"

"Welcome to the sticks, pal."

"Why don't we just go to the Louisiana side? I'll bet there's a hotel around there."

"We don't have time for that. I think I saw an apartment complex back there. Maybe they've got something open."

"No time, huh? Well, you better pull out Uncle Sam's credit card, 'cause *I* sure as hell ain't payin' for it."

The two find an unoccupied apartment to hole up in: the model unit. It's already furnished with basic items, all colored ruby red, with the typical cheap art decor covering the walls. It's all a bit too gaudy for either of them, but the simple convenience brings a morsel of satisfaction to the two irritable men. Using false identities and a bit of sweet talking, the two are able to secure a same day move in and set up shop in the two-bedroom apartment. Afterward, Reed suggests they find a place to get some food. The choice is made easy as there's only one diner in the whole town, and it's nearby. Everything is nearby in Brayerville.

The two enter the modest diner and are seated by a very nice but visibly exhausted young lady. Her charm and Southern vernacular bring a smile to Reed's face, a fact that serves only to irritate Bourke. The place looks like the most basic example of an American diner that one could come across. White walls, red booths, and a dash of despair. They order their meals and almost immediately start picking at one another. Bourke starts in, first.

"So, you're a priest, right?

"I was."

"Hmph... I've never been one for livin' my life by dusty books and other people's words."

In a moment of confusion at the sudden jab, Reed's eyes linger on Bourke before he responds, "Is that right? Well, that's great, pal. It must be something special to have perfect confidence in your own opinions."

"Yeah, it feels pretty good. Never had to look to someone else for mine."

Reed nods with an empty crocodile smile. "Yessir, you've got it all figured out. That's great. But some people don't have your immense natural gifts, ya know? Some people need guidance. The word is there to give that guidance, and I was there to facilitate it."

Now with a firm tone, Bourke jabs back. "Yeah? It ever fix anybody, *pal*? Or did it just give you a sense of purpose?"

"What's your problem? You have issues or something?"

Bourke scoffs and lights a cigarette.

Reed points to the ceiling, alluding to the fact that they're inside. "Really?"

"What, you gonna harp on my health? Fuck off, I smoke. Deal with it."

"Right. I will have to deal with it if we come up against just one pyromancer and you get your face flash cooked... idiot."

"We're not chasin' a pyromancer, asshole. It's just some old dude who likes to choke people. I don't even know why we're needed out here." Bourke flicks cigarette ash into his coffee mug with disdain and stares out the large glass diner window, elbow hanging off the back of his booth bench.

"You were briefed just like I was, Bourke. We're here because they're certain it's a possession. Hence, why you have to put up with my righteous ass."

Before the scene can escalate any further, their contentious stares are interrupted by the chiming sound of the doorbell as an especially ripe vagabond shuffles into the diner. Bourke shifts his eyes to the man and leans to look over Reed's shoulder as the man enters behind him. A grimace permeates Bourke's face. The wait staff is none too welcoming and proceed to gently but insistently shew the man until the waitress gets him to leave.

Bourke exclaims, "Fuckin' hillbillies, man. They make me nervous."

Reed responds with a curled lip, "You hunt monsters for a living, and you're worried about southerners?"

"You ever seen that one movie? I'm not about to be anyone's little piggy. Hell no, not me."

Reed simply peels back a half-cocked smirk while shaking his head and lets it be. After their meal, the two are more than ready to be done with occupying a booth together. They tip well and leave to investigate the location where the body was found.

The agents drive to the riverbank, approximately where the body was discovered, just south of Brayerville, west of the rural community of Ellesburrow. Reed walks around the vehicle and retrieves from the trunk of their car a PERMA (Paranormal Exploration, Research & Management Agency) device, called an aura sensor, to read any suspicious supernatural energy levels in the area.

"What's that?" Bourke asks.

"Are you serious?" Bourke raises his eyebrows... "You're serious. It's an aura sensor." Bourke simply shrugs and looks off into the distance. "Never used one."

"It's standard issue. How've you nev—look, it just reads energy levels. Speaking of, I think I've got something."

The reading reveals abnormally high levels of ectoplasmic radiation. The reading suggests the area is indeed active with some sort of ethereal entity. The presence of water prevents a more thorough scan of the location, but Reed posits that they're certainly somewhere close, due to the readings he gets.

"The water is stunting the sensor a bit, but there's definitely something going on here. These readings are fairly strong, especially for the middle of nowhere."

"Guess we're on the right track, then. Looks like your little toy is worth somethin', after all."

Reed stares up the bank and points with two fingers. "I think we should walk north and see if the readings change. I'm betting they will."

"Huh? I'm not walkin' the bank with you, like a couple o' tourists. It's hot as shit out here, anyway. I can feel my own breath bouncing off the air, it's so thick. I'm going back to the car."

Bourke starts to walk back to their car and turns to Reed. "You coming?"

Reed's eyes are fixed on the device in his hands. "No, you go ahead. I'm gonna do my job."

"Whatever," Bourke retorts, and returns to the car. He drives off, leaving Reed to track the readings on his own. Reed walks the bank of the Mississippi, using the aura sensor to read as he goes. His walk is a bit tense, with the thought of a killer popping out at any moment sitting forefront in his mind, but the walk is uneventful. He walks along the bank for about an hour, making it back to Brayerville on foot. Reed, soaked from head to toe in sweat, gets back to the apartment to find Bourke passed out on the couch with the remnants of what looks to have been quite a feast strewn about: mostly takeout from the diner. Trash and empty wrappers pepper the living space. On the counter, next to an empty cup, Reed sees a bottle of pills. Reed stares at his "partner" as Bourke snores loudly, drool seeping into his pillow.

Reed is hungry, but just lets out a disappointed sigh and disregards the thoughtless display. He turns and sits down at the cheaply made kitchen table to think. The table isn't level and wobbles whenever weight is put on it, making an irritating rattling noise. Bourke wakes up from his self-induced food coma to see Reed writing at the table. The rickety furniture knocks back and forth as he works.

"Reed? Made it back, huh? What're you doin'?"

"Working."

Bourke wipes the sleep from his eyes and sits up. "Do you always have your nose in a case?"

"What, you don't study the facts?"

Bourke walks over to the empty chair opposite Reed, nonchalantly burps and sits down. "Eh... not really. They send me to take somethin' down—I take it down." Bourke gestures a gun with his fingers and continues, "My gun usually does the work just fine." He leans back in his chair with a raised brow, leisurely watching Reed sift through papers.

"So, what's the biggest fucker you've ever taken down?"

Reed, only barely paying attention, eyes still flipping and scanning through notes like a 1930s accountant, "Uhh, wereboar. You?"

"I put down a mire troll one time. Sunuvabitch was probably two tons." Bourke's inflection and tone signify a not so thinly veiled hubris in his words.

Now, paying enough attention to measure feats with Bourke, Reed replies. "Well, size isn't everything, pal. I captured a Kill Trust assassin a couple years back."

"No shit? Which one?"

"Killstreak."

"That was you? Wait, didn't he escape?"

"Yeah... but that wasn't on me. I just turn them in. After that, it's out of my hands."

"Damn. How'd you manage to take him in, anyway? Isn't he supposed to be crazy fast?"

"Yeah, the fastest I've ever seen. I got him talking—hit him with a ricochet."

"Heh. I knew those mandatory physics classes would come in handy, somehow."

The two continue to talk and bond a little more over the case.

"So, like I thought, the readings were much higher the closer I got to town," Reed says.

"You think the killer's livin' in town?"

"I'm not sure. Possibly."

Both of them are somewhat anxious, feeling as though they're starting to close in. Reed decides to leave it alone for the night and get some rest. He gets up from the table and walks toward the bathroom hallway.

"I'm gonna get a shower and hit the sack. I smell like a wet dog." Reed stops and hesitates before turning halfway to look at Bourke. "Those pills over there… those a problem?

Bourke glances back at the counter. "Naw, man. Just… my head gets a little full, sometimes. Only way I can sleep when it's bad. The food helps."

Reed's guard drops a bit, as if the bout of honesty disarms him. "Yeah, I understand. The job weighs heavy. It can all be a bit much, at times. Sorry to pry."

"No worries. By the way, man, there's some food in the fridge for you."

Reed looks at Bourke with a surprised expression.

Bourke recognizes the look and playfully jabs at Reed. "What, you didn't think I was that much of a dick, did you?"

Reed responds, "Of course not, pal."

The following day, the agents wake to a commotion going on outside the apartment. Reed is the first to rise from the grip of sleep and sit up. He stumbles to the door in a half sleep with a weary hesitance and looks through the peephole before opening the door. Outside lays a body, sprawled out in the parking lot of the apartments. Residents and local sheriffs are gathered around. Bourke comes to the door, peering over Reed's shoulder to examine the scenery, taking note of the body: a woman.

"Is that…" Bourke pauses.

Reed confirms Bourke's suspicions. "Yeah... the waitress from the diner." The two watch for a moment before quietly closing the door. Reed stands just on the inside of the closed door, his hand still gripping the knob, then turns and looks at Bourke with a restrained but remorseful countenance. The two are not sure if it is a message for them, or just a terrible coincidence. In any case, they decide to get to work immediately following the unfortunate start to the day.

Reed informs his partner of the location which garnered the heaviest reading from the aura sensor on his walk the day prior. Still making an attempt not to stand out, they both don their inconspicuous attire and make the short drive to the bank of the Mississippi, where Reed had left off. Reed breaks out the aura sensor and leans over to show Bourke the reading on the device's screen. "You see that? This reading is much higher than the surrounding areas. There's something about this particular spot."

Bourke glances at the screen and back at the ground where they stand. Suddenly, something grabs Bourke's attention. He walks over to a peculiar bundle of brush, kicking it aside. "Well, lookey there," he says, "Someone's trying to hide their tracks." Under the brush is freshly disturbed ground—tracks of some sort.

Reed inquisitively walks over and squats down to get a better look. He pans his head back and forth from the tracks to the water a few times and shakes his finger toward the river bank. "These are boat tracks. Someone's been dragging a small boat through here. You're right, they've tried to hide this with the brush lying around."

Bourke postulates, "A bit odd since there's docs up and down the bank, don't ya think?"

Reed stands and looks around. "Yeah, I do. This spot's through the trees, away from prying eyes... I can't imagine that's for nothing."

As the two kick around the spot, Bourke pipes up with an observation. "Hey, what about those islands out there?"

Reed crosses his arms and stares out over the water before

responding. "The river islands… there's several up and down the Mississippi."

"And with no one to call 'em home."

"These tracks are from a boat coming and going *across* the river, not down. I'll be damned. Looks like we've got some boating to do, pal."

The two Blue Coats wait until nightfall, this time suiting up in full gear, at this point giving little thought to spooking the killer, especially in the cloak of night. Blue Coats are distinctive in their attire. The deep blue highwayman-like long coats they wear are lined in silver trim, providing a striking visage resembling colonial gunslingers. Some wear hats of various types. Neither Bourke nor Reed are the sort. They do, however, wear well-stocked ammo belts: a veritable carousel of silver and lead. Their coats are dense and slash-proof, not a typical fabric of fashion. With the donning of their uniform, so dons their hunter's state of mind.

They grab a boat from the small docks on the bank and take it to the tracks they'd found, making their way across the river, to the island directly opposite the bank. As they approach, Reed is taking readings with the aura sensor. The readings spike, as Reed expected. When the two of them get to the bank of the island, their noses are assaulted with an almighty stench. It's faint at the bank, but gets much more fetid as they venture into the trees peppering the island.

They walk into the brush and foliage, using the sensor to track the spiking energy signature. Suddenly Bourke puts his hand on Reed's chest, stopping him in his tracks. "Get your eyes off that screen and look up." Bourke points ahead; through the trees is a makeshift shanty situated among the trees and dirt. The structure looks abandoned at first glance, but as the agents begin to move closer, they can see the signs of activity.

"This *could* just be a homeless camp," Reed says.

"That stench is something more than stinking hobos, Reed," Bourke replies, shaking his head defiantly.

The two move in on the structure, stopping just outside as both pull their guns. Bourke and Reed are each brandishing a stainless-steel SRA issue six-shot fifty-cal revolver: standard weapons of Blue Coats—and one that creates a lump in the throat of most who behold the silver sheen. Every Blue Coat is equipped with special kinetic-dampening wrist bracers to handle the powerful recoil and trained in quick draw techniques, along with a form of close quarters combat specifically tailored to complement their skills and equipment. They can draw their weapon and blast a hole through a concrete wall in a split second.

Bourke starts walking toward the front of the shanty, while Reed circles around back, weapons at the ready. The two converge and enter from their respective sides with no resistance, only to see the horror of the scene inside.

The shanty is clearly a kill house. The two holster their weapons and walk around the defiled space, looking for any identifying information, either of the killer or the victims. They find nothing but signs of struggle, along with some handheld weapons and an unsettling amount of bodily fluids, excrement and filth. "This killer must be into more than just strangulation. This place is downright grisly," says Reed. Bourke nods and takes a half step toward a heavily bloodstained wooden table that's nestled in the far corner of the shanty, placing his hand on the surface. Reed isn't paying attention to Bourke until he hears a low moan come from his partner. Reed snaps around to see Bourke, hand still placed on the table, hanging his head backward with eyes rolled back in his head. Alarmed, Reed starts to walk over to him, stopping when Bourke begins to speak.

"No... just... let me see." Bourke exhales a long breath and begins to see a vivid vision. He sees the killer, standing inside the moonlit shanty but obscured by shadow, talking to another person. The person is a young lady. She's tied to the wooden table, strapped down, unable to move. The killer is looming over the girl and brandishing a dirty cleaver, speaking to her with a minacious growl.

"Amputation… now, that's a skill. Dismemberment? That's easy enough. Anyone can hack at flesh until it comes free. But to take your limbs from you, one by one… and to do it with skill… you see, that's what I bring to the butcher's block. And rest assured, I will apply all of my abilities to your torture. You are in very capable hands. Now, let's get started."

The woman squirms and shrieks through a gag, unable to do anything to escape or avoid the killer's actions. As the cleaver is viciously brought downward, into the young woman's flesh, Bourke lets out a sharp yelp and stumbles backward a few steps, breaking out of the vision. Reed braces his partner and looks at him with confusion. "You have the gift of psychometry?" Reed asks.

Bourke responds while shaking his head free of the cobwebs and kneading his brow, "Yeah… so?"

With a slight snicker, Reed says, "Nothing. I just didn't know. No wonder you don't need an aura sensor."

"Yeah. But that's why I do need the pills, sometimes. Shit makes my head spin."

After Bourke explains what he saw, Reed is understandably disturbed. The two aren't sure if the killer was a surgeon or a butcher, or maybe just simply deranged. Reed walks out the back door that he'd entered through and stares into the trees surrounding the area, thinking to himself. He then begins talking to Bourke while still peering outside. "Well, what now? We could set up shop and wait. There's no guarantee anyone will come back here, though—

"Bourke?" Reed looks back over his shoulder and sees Bourke shuttering, taking one step forward into the moonlight that pierces the makeshift shanty. Reed calls out one more time as he places his hand on his revolver, "Bourke…"

As Bourke steps forward, Reed's eyes widen as he takes in the sight and yells, "*Bourke!*" Bourke has a pair of shears protruding from his throat. As the shears are violently ripped from his throat, Bourke is left gargling as he falls to his knees, clenching his throat with his hands to keep the wound closed. Just behind Bourke, standing in the doorway of the shack, is a silhouetted figure. Reed is unable to make out exactly who it is, but it does appear to be humanoid.

Being some of the most highly trained members of the SRA, Blue Coats endure repetitive drills and practice under pressure, for split second occasions much like this, and that training kicks in. Reed pulls his glaring steel revolver with peak human speed and efficiency and manages to get off a single powerful shot toward the hidden figure, grazing it in the arm before it quickly bolts away, somewhere outside the structure. If it'd been a solid shot, that arm would be hamburger meat, but the figure moved with unnatural reflexes, outdoing the Blue Coat's precision and speed.

Reed thinks quickly and forgoes chasing the figure, instead moving to shut the back door and secure the front. The two are sitting ducks inside that shanty, but Bourke is in bad shape. Reed looks around for anything potentially useful to doctor Bourke's wounds while simultaneously attempting to calm and comfort his partner, but everything is filthy and completely unsuitable. "Hold on, buddy!" With Bourke resting on his knees, Reed takes off his long coat and tries to use it to stop the bleeding from his throat. "You're doing great, Bourke. Hold on." But the efficacy of his approach is questionable. Bourke's wounds are grave, indeed.

Reed tries to address the neck wound, but the wound gushes blood whenever Bourke's hands are removed from his throat. He feels helpless, watching his partner hold his throat closed while he quickly bleeds to death, growing paler by the second.

The horrid feeling is interrupted by a raspy voice shouting from outside. It is the killer—the man who's been possessed. "You can't save him. You can't save anyone."

Bourke gestures for Reed to come closer. He clutches Reed's shirt and, with great effort, quietly tells Reed, "Get... him."

Reed places his hand on Bourke's shoulder and gets up to bar the back door of the shanty, then walks out the front door. "I'll be back, just hang on, Bourke," says Reed before shutting the door tightly behind him.

Reed then walks a few paces outside the shanty, takes a deep breath and pulls his sidearm. The moonlight casts piercing rays through the softly rustling trees around the wooded river island, gleaming off the polished steel pistol and creating a juxtaposed atmosphere of calming anxiety. The man begins to taunt Reed while dashing between trees in bursts of unnatural movement. Reed thinks back to his encounter with the fleet-footed Kill Trust assassin he'd captured years earlier. He quickly formulates a plan, deciding to engage with the killer while he tries to nail down a pattern of movement. *Let's start with the obvious questions and get this bastard talking,* he thinks to himself.

"Who are you?" Reed asks.

"I am a lost soul. I am no one now. I... am the consequence."

"All right. Jack, it is. Why are you killing people, Jack?"

"Punishment," the man responds.

The man suddenly becomes still... momentarily, before disappearing just as quickly. Reed's eyes dart around the trees, looking for Jack but sees nothing. Then, out of nowhere, Reed is hit with a sharp pain in his thigh. He yells out and looks down to see a slash in his leg. Jack had dashed by, slicing him with a blade or sharp object of some sort.

Jack then speaks again. "Humans are nasty and hateful. They are cruel! They torture and terrorize those who are weak or different. But they insist on pushing until they can push no more. They often forget that even worms will turn."

"Oh, cry me another river. People were mean to you, so you kill them? Maybe they were right!"

"I am still here because I have a purpose. I am the consequence!"

"Yeah, I heard you the first time. You sound more like a whiny child to me." Reed is slashed again, this time in the back of the leg. "Ahh! Shit! You're really pushing my priestly patience, pal!"

Reed is hit with several more slashes, in succession. His back, legs, and arms are bleeding profusely from the wounds. *Damn it*, he thinks to himself, *Of course he slashes at me while I don't have my coat on. In the dark, no less.* Reed, fighting the pain, backs up to the shanty, literally putting his back to the wall, hoping to give himself some protection from the slashes coming from behind. As he stands, propped up against the wall, bleeding, Jack appears directly in front of him, startling Reed. With a deafening sound, five shots ring out from the .500 caliber pistol… but not from Reed's.

One more shot follows, then silence. "Bourke…" Reed's eyes shift to the side, then to the ground in realization of what had happened. His gravely injured partner had ended his pain. It sounded to Reed like he emptied his clip, presumably so as not to leave a loaded weapon for the killer. "I guess you were more chivalrous than I gave you credit for, buddy," Reed says quietly.

The sudden event has Reed swimming in his own head. *Damn it all! Alright… I can't let this possessed piece of garbage get away with that. Concentrate.* He begins to breathe deep and focus. *C'mon, look for a pattern. You've done this before.* The dark spirit-corrupted killer is still playing a sick game of peekaboo. Reed takes two more slashes to his torso, but this time he doesn't flinch. He ignores the pain and tries to zero in on the killer's movements, controlling his breathing and keeping his hand steady. Then, *"Now!"* Reed draws quickly and fires a dead-eye shot, nailing Jack in the leg with his high-powered sidearm as Jack dashes by. The shot causes the swift killer to stumble, but he doesn't yell or howl in pain. *I know that had to damn near blow his knee apart*, Reed thinks.

The killer attempts to dash by again, seemingly undeterred by the high caliber gunshot wound to his leg, but Reed is able to dodge the now impaired assailant. There is a lull, before the killer changes tactics and appears behind Reed, who has moved away from the shanty while dodging. Jack quickly wraps a boat line around Reed's neck, cinching it tightly and dragging him to the ground, causing Reed to drop his sidearm. The two struggle as the man wrenches the rope, grunting and heaving, digging it further into Reed's trachea. As his head spins and his eyeballs feel as though they're trying to escape a fire inside his skull, Reed knows he has little time before he passes out. Thankfully, although the man has supernatural movement and speed, his strength is within normal human range.

The rope burns as it constricts his throat, but Reed thinks quickly. With all his might, he violently jerks his body to the side, turning into his attacker, pushing his weight into him, alleviating the pressure on his throat. With the rope now pulling into the back of his head, Reed is unable to see; his face pressed against the man's chest, he's forced to inhale the musky stench emanating from his unwashed torso.

Even though he's no longer being choked, the bastard just won't let loose. Reed reaches up to find the man's face and begins repeatedly smashing his fist into it. The most unsettling thing about the situation is the laughter coming from the possessed madman. He's completely unaffected by the pummeling. He just continues to laugh maniacally. Reed reaches back, grabbing the hands of his attacker and manages to peel Jack's grip away, pulling his head out and freeing himself from the hold. The scramble that ensues is a blur. Even if asked to recount the event, Reed wouldn't know how to explain just how he managed what came next.

The two scramble to get an edge over the other, like two starved dogs fighting for scraps. And at the end of it, Reed recovers his revolver, with the man directly in his sights. As the possessed killer dives down at Reed with something clutched between his two hands, Reed fires a single shot, striking the man in the head. The fifty caliber blast from the gun rings Reed's ears and obliterates the man's skull, sending fragments of bone and flesh soaring, and any last thoughts along with it.

As Reed lies on the ground, motionless, his arm still outstretched, pointing his gun in the air, he realizes the man he had been fighting was the "vagabond" from the diner. It's nearly impossible to recognize him now, half a head and all, but that was definitely his murderous mug grimacing at Reed moments before. Either way, the Higher-Ups aren't going to be happy about the results... at all. Reed gathers himself, feeling the effects of the multiple slashes and cuts on his body, his Adam's apple still throbbing, he prepares to make the solemn journey back to SRA headquarters to deliver bad news to his superiors—sans his partner, Bourke. Reed lets out a heavy sigh and begins the process of wrestling with his anxiety. "I always look forward to this part," he mumbles sarcastically, to himself. He's sure now it will be even worse with not only one, but two bodies on his hands. No matter the circumstances, Reed knows this case isn't over... yet. He's still got to own up.

Back at SRA HQ, Reed sits in an uncomfortable bare metal folding chair, awaiting the brutal grilling he's about to receive. He thinks to himself while he sits silently. *I always hated the smell of this place. Like old dusty carpet and warm electronics. Feels like I'm waiting for the principal to call me in.*

Reed, staring at his feet, hears the debriefing agent call his name. The debriefing area is lined with unending fluorescent lights; and not the overtly bright soul sucking kind, but the kind that's so old and dirty it's developed a crusty interior, making each light dim and flickery. It's a perfect place to berate someone into submission. And that they did. They hit all the important points: the failure to exorcise the spirit, failure to capture said spirit, the death of Bourke, the whole list. They covered the entirety of the failures incurred by the case while Reed, just slightly slumped in his chair, listens, unable to defend himself. Their disappointment in the vessel being dead is very clear, even more so that Reed, of all people, was the culprit.

"This is the *very* result we sent you to prevent," said the furious Balecrest. The debriefing agent looked on with a discernible amount of disappointment and a sour expression on his face. Reed can do nothing but hang his head and accept responsibility. Though, he can't help but feel that Belecrest is more infuriated by not having a test subject for his experimental torture device. The machine is supposedly meant for ethereal entities—apparently a PERMA (Paranormal Exploration, Research, and Management Agency) creation—and something many had heard rumblings about. But what's done is done. The spirit, Jack, was loose in the ether, unaccounted for, and most likely poised to possess another unsuspecting soul.

Once his superiors were done letting him know how bad he'd screwed up, Reed exited the dank debriefing office and headed nowhere in particular. The death was heavy. All of it. His former life as a priest was frequently heavy, as well. But carrying the burden of confessional knowledge isn't quite the same as bearing the weight of death; one that you can't help but somehow feel responsible for.

As Reed solemnly walks to the exit and the midday sun splashes upon his face, pulling his eyelids closer together, he thinks to himself, *I left the life of a priest for this. I remember like it was yesterday, the logic I clung to. I told myself, 'I can settle to console people, or I can truly save people.' The choice seemed easy, then. Now, I'm not so sure. This world is sharp on all edges. Choices are never as simple as they seem. If this has taught me anything, it's that death is not the worst thing that can happen in this life, just the most. The afterlife... that's another story.*

THE NIGHTMARE
BY ALI LAUDERDALE

In the somber solitude of the night, I found myself entrusted with the emergency care of a child, a cherub of innocence, in a house as old as the hills. Her mother, with a heavy heart, found herself obliged to attend a gathering of the townsfolk, summoned by some unidentified pressure, rendering her unable to be absent from the event.

I engaged in playful diversions with the small girl for a span of time, yet presently I consigned her to sleep. I found no peculiarity in the child's predilection for slumbering within the mother's bed. I speculated that she merely yearned for her sole living parent.

The ticking of an ancient clock echoed through the silence, a lullaby to my weary senses. Once the little girl had succumbed to unconsciousness, I cast my gaze upon the timeworn abode. A modest edifice, it possessed a dual-tiered arrangement, united by a wrought-iron spiral staircase. The top level manifested as an improved attic, with a pair of chambers. Every grown person was compelled to bow beneath the oppressive weight of the abysmally inclined, cathedral-like canopy. In the domicile, scarcely any furnishings adorned each room, yet in the loft, a dearth of such articles prevailed. The chamber stretched forth, its length seemingly endless, and within its confines resided naught but a decrepit, weathered pallet. In my specific musings, I deemed it most peculiar to repose upon the dusty couch below, thusly I endeavored to procure a modest coverlet and nestled myself to dormancy within the vacant chamber, whereupon that solitary mattress lay.

As I ascended the winding steps, a recollection seized my mind, like a specter haunting the corridors of my thoughts. It was the tale of my dear companion, who dwelt within this abode, and spoke of that room nestled in the highest echelon of this dwelling. She'd confessed, with a tremor in her voice, that an unspoken dread had taken root within her heart, rendering her fearful of dozing in that very chamber. I had chuckled softly unto myself, as she had been unable to expound upon the reason wherefore, which was the very cause for my dismissal of her trepidation as naught but folly.

The pallid glow of the external streetlamp permeated the undulating panes of age-worn glass. The gloomy hue of the infantile azure pigment of the walls commingled with the morbid luminescence, casting a crushing weight upon the atmosphere. Yet, I deemed it necessary to surrender to somnolence, thus I shut my weary eyes and fell to the abyss.

In the depths of an indeterminate hour, I found myself bound in a desperate battle for breath. Simultaneously, I perceived myself endeavoring to ascend from slumber's clutches akin to one struggling amidst the treacherous grip of quicksand. A ponderous burden lay upon my bosom, and with each labored exhalation, the inhalation of breath grew more arduous. When roused from my slumber, I mustered all my might to partake in the laborious task of unveiling my weary eyes, an exhausting effort that consumed both my vigor and an inescapable span of time.

The chamber was enveloped in a ghastly moonbeam, which bestowed upon it an otherworldly discoloration. A lengthy, grotesque silhouette capered upon the walls with a macabre grace. That somber shadow was cast by a towering specter that loomed over my trembling body. It possessed an undeniably masculine essence, yet there existed naught of humanity within its being. My solitary thought did naught but ascertain the presence of a malevolent spirit. 'Twas the figure of a man, yet the semblance ceased to exist beyond that. The corporeal form, shrouded in ethereal obscurity, bore an essence of pure, inky darkness. Countless wormy tendrils, sinuous and sharp, adorned its visage, while jagged ebony horns protruded from the entirety. Though my sight beheld no eyes on the creature, I sensed a spectral gaze fixated upon me. Though it did not strive to touch me, I realized it to be the very cause of my labored respiration.

In a flash, I perceived I was ensnared by an icy grip that penetrated the very depths of my being. Quivering tremors traversed the length of my spine, sending a chill through my core. How was I to elude the clutches of this malevolent thing? When I endeavored to shift my body(whose mortality I was increasingly becoming aware), I identified a most harrowing revelation: I was ensnared in the clutches of a merciless paralysis, utterly bereft of volition. This did naught but augment my trepidation. The noxious scent of petroleum jelly and sulfur enveloped me, its corrosive tendrils constricting my lungs, rendering each breath a more exhausting endeavor than before. In the depths of despair, I beheld my sole glimmer of salvation, a flickering ember amidst the encroaching darkness. It lay in the distant recesses of my consciousness, which was whispering a frantic cry for deliverance. A door, previously concealed within the opposing wall, beckoned me with its siren song, enticing an escape to the world beyond. An external staircase possibly awaited my fleeting footsteps. A grave anguish befell me as I exerted every fiber of my muscles, yet alas, I remained immobilized, with the malevolent specter leering over me.

I struggled 'gainst the unseen fetters, my heart throbbing within my chest. That ominous shadow form was gazing upon me, and a tormenting ache seized hold of my skull. I could sense the frigid exhalation, perceive the putrid and strangely sweet odor of decomposition. I found myself ensnared within the confines of my own corporeal vessel, compelled to endure this ghastly torment that plagued my every waking moment.

I was drenched in a frigid perspiration, as I exerted every ounce of my strength against the intangible shackles, under the undeniable dominion of the demonic creature. The very notion that it remained motionless did naught but instill within me a profound dread. Its hushed stillness reflected the entirety of my existence on that ancient mattress. Then I recollected the tiny child slumbering in her mother's chamber beneath me. Whate'er this creature's vile intent, I knew full well its cruel design would not cease with me alone, but extend its wicked grasp upon the tender frame of the innocent girl once its designs had been sated upon my wretched soul. The notion of the child enduring the same affliction as I did imbued me with an urgency to exert myself amidst the agony, and, by sheer force of will, I succeeded in painstakingly turning my body over.

I tumbled from the drab mattress, landing at the horrific creature's feet, its visage mirroring the grim consistency that pervaded its entire presence. In an instant, it stirred. Without the slightest shake of its limbs, it translocated mere paces from me, yet obstinately obstructed the threshold to the winding staircase.

I resolved that the far exit to the outside world was but a distant prospect, and moreover, an air of foreboding clung to that very threshold. I noticed that it throbbed in the eerie luminosity, nearly alive in a spectral glow.

Alighting upon the floor appeared to invigorate my muscles, and albeit akin to grudgingly traversing a quagmire, I gradually mustered the strength to propel my arms forth. I clutched the cold, unyielding floor, my fingers digging into its unforgiving surface. With every ounce of strength I possessed, I endeavored to drag my weary body across the desolate expanse toward the staircase. It seemed eternally did the infernal entity bear witness, whilst a somber reverberation swelled within my ears, and my skull yet pulsated. Never before had I known such a chilling fright, as if the very distillate of dread had seeped into the marrow of my bones, leaving an indelible mark upon my soul.

Quivering, I persisted in an ungainly and whimpering army crawl along the cold surface beneath the vigilant stare of the abomination. I anticipated its imminent assault upon me, yet the nature of its nefarious designs upon my prone form remained shrouded in enigmatic obscurity. Might I, perchance, be ensnared within the clutches of an infernal abyss? Might it, likely, engulf and torment my poor body? The possibilities knocked upon my very bones.

The sole source of fortitude bestowed upon my fatigued spirit was the contemplation of the innocent girl sleeping below, cocooned within her blissful reveries, oblivious to the imminent danger lurking in the room above her. I dragged myself past the foul creature, and I discovered my movements improved upon reaching the staircase of wrought-iron. I made an effort to elevate my self, that I might scoot down the steps. As I ventured forth, distancing myself from the chamber, the resounding clamor and repugnant odor gradually waned. I was consumed by an apprehension so grave that I dared not cast my gaze upon the haunted chamber behind me.

Upon reaching the ground level, a lingering anxiety clung to my core, yet the realm before me appeared to have returned to its mundane state. The fetor and the resonance had dissipated, and though my malaise persisted, I regained the ability to mobilize, respire, and traverse with customary ease. My heart brimming with gratitude, I traversed the somber chamber, until I found solace upon the moth-eaten couch. The hush within the dwelling was void, and once more I perceived the consoling constancy of the ticking timepiece.

Alas, I did not give in to restful sleep for the remainder of that eve. Instead, I kept a vigilant watch over the slumbering child, lest the fiendish entity should dare to ensnare her in its wicked grasp. I was ignorant of the means by which I might vanquish it, should it dare to assail her, yet I was resolute in my determination to make the attempt. I fixated upon the blessed act of respiration, and held dear every single breath.

Never had I felt such profound thankfulness for the warm and radiant orb in the sky as I did on that defining morning, when the mother of the girl at last made her long-awaited return. I bade farewell and departed from that accursed abode, vowing nevermore to cross its threshold. Later, upon beholding my companion, who had confessed she trembled at the thought of falling asleep within that very chamber where I had encountered that evil, I simply inclined my head in solemn acquiescence. We had no need for discourse; for within our hearts lay the mournful verity that eludes the grasp of ordinary souls. Whether dream or wakefulness, forever shall I be haunted by the recollection of that fateful eve. In the ethereal realm betwixt slumber and consciousness, we are at the mercy of our own nightmares.

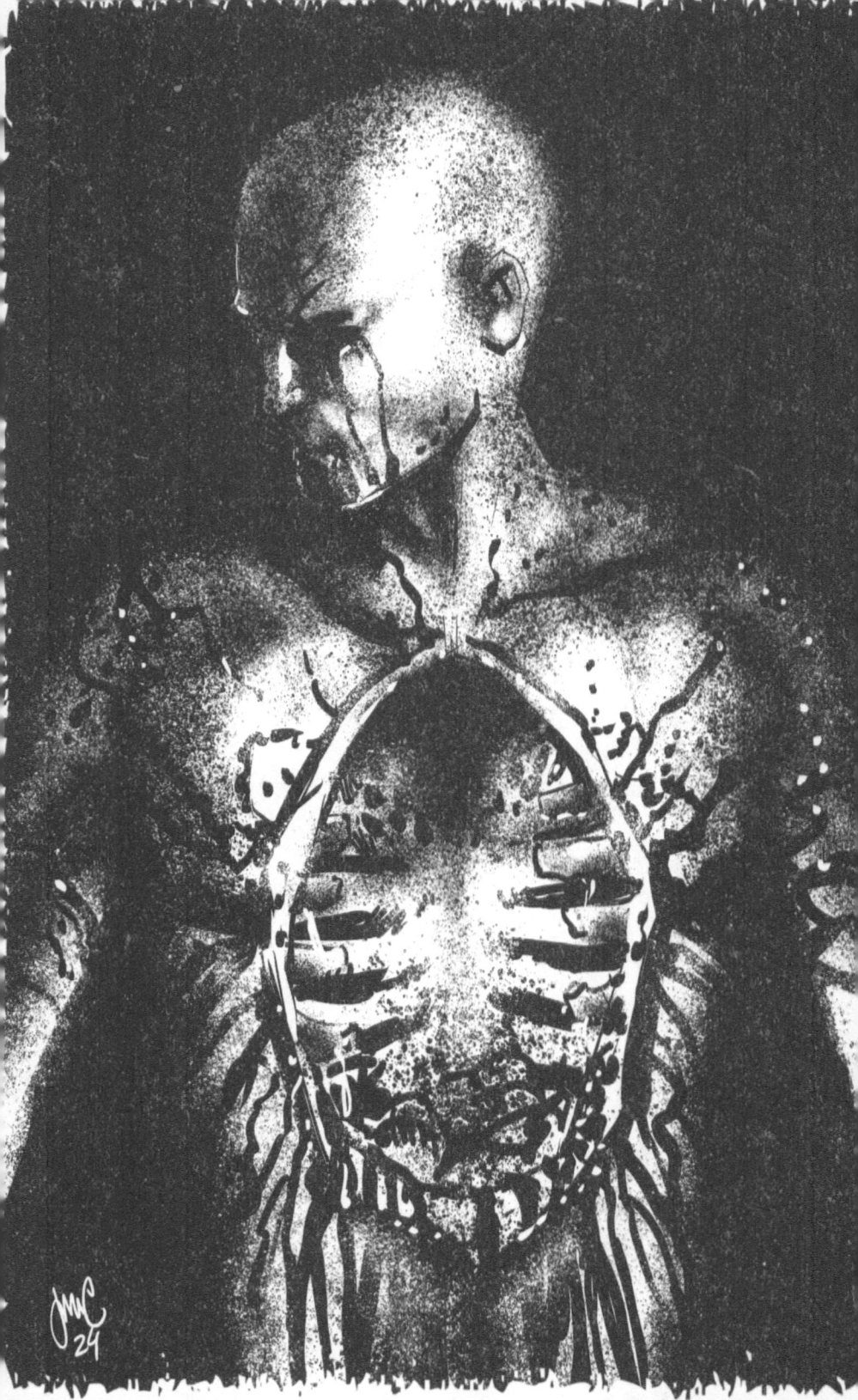

ARCHIVE

BY NARWHAL

The charge was released, and the transport took place. Archive stepped off the platform, now in 2-D space. His eyes no longer worked, so he closed them. The guard handed him a special viewfinder to interface with, which allowed him to get bearings on his surroundings, so that when the guard said, "Follow me," Archive knew what direction to move.

The information of his 3-Dimensional being had been zipped, ready for him when he returned, like leaving a coat at Coat Check, and he ventured forth in his new form. 2-D space felt more "floaty," and mirrors didn't work or even exist. To him, it was like playing an old video game on the Famicom, with the top down view of a castle at his fingertips.

It took a certain amount of time to get to any point, just like in 3-D space. Someone might have to grab a key first, but it is possible. However, time marches on nonetheless. That was one of Archive's problems.

"If only there was a world where time stood still," he thought, "something like a pause menu or an inventory screen."

As he learned more about the dimensions, he was eventually able to confirm for himself what every hobo and billionaire on Earth in any of the three dimensions would have told him if he gave them a dollar and asked for advice: it's all about time. And when it comes to time, there's no free lunch, no cheating, no stealing, and no trading.

Time progressing across dimensions universally was the thing that made it possible for them to travel "in-between" in the first place. *At least I don't have to fetch a key,* he thought.

The problem was that a donut-shaped cut of the city, back in 3-D space, had been laser-baked.

A great floating beacon had appeared at the top of the Nakatomi building. Anyone within eyesight of the thing had their ribcage explode. About 1,800 people were killed. Then another thousand more died before people figured out not to enter the "donut zone."

Calling it a donut wasn't exactly accurate. It was more like a bagel; the 'hole' was very small. The destructive beacon had a root, like tributaries of a river or nerve endings, growing beneath it, that extended below into the top floors of the Nakatomi Building. These roots delineated a bubble of safety, extending out from the beacon with a radius of about 150 feet. No one within that bubble had their ribcage explode, but now they were hostages.

"Archive!" The king of the 2-D kingdom of Monze called. "To what do I owe the pleasure?"

This was Archive's second stop, so he already had some information to work with to formulate useful questions. "Did you torture a 2nd-Dimensional beast of immeasurable power and release it into the third dimension?"

The king stood. "Okay, first off, I didn't release it. It was stolen. And, as for the torture, that was the zoo; that wasn't me; that wasn't even in our dimension when that happened. And I wouldn't even call it torture; it's just how animals don't like to be imprisoned; you know how it is." The king had heard about what had happened already.

"Okay, how do I stop it?"

"Beats me, old sport. What happened? It was those bastard Pings who took it. I haven't gotten around to slapping them back for it." In truth, the King had lost interest in his latest pet, and he had sold it to the Pings, to whom the creature was still quite exotic and fascinating.

Archive cursed the fact that he had to make another stop. "Can I talk to it?"

"You don't have direct experience?"

"I'm documenting as I go."

"If you get close enough, yeah. It's not like talking to a tree or anything. It's more like talking to a ghost."

"Can it understand me?"

"If you imitate my voice and language, it will understand."

Archive had the king's data on deck. He turned. He had a theory already, but he needed to speak to the Pings. "It's angry."

"Archive, where are you going? Won't you stay for a cup of tea?"

Archive ignored him, which in Monze was an act of war. But the king decided to let this one go, and enjoyed a cup of tea by himself.

The Beacon Creature was called a Dordent. In low gravity, it resembled one of Nikola Tesla's experiments, with roots shooting out in all directions like electric strands. But on Earth, the roots spun and twined downward. Archive was able to identify it with a telescope. They didn't call him 'Archive' for nothing.

Dordents were passed and bred among kings and collected in 2-D space. But moving them to 3-D space was obviously dangerous, and ripping out parts of them that would have been zipped if they were 3-D going 2-D, but going the other way, the process was reverse engineered. This effectively created something out of nothing. For most 2-D beings, the process was still stable. But for Dordents, anything could happen.

It's like rolling dice for stats on a unique item in a children's game, Archive thought to himself. If dealers were farming Dordents into 3-D space, they would rip them into a space without other living beings around.

You could technically rip them into populated 3-D space as an act of war, a powerful weapon. But why would the 2-D and 3-D realms fight? A vendetta had been settled here or there, a romantic rivalry, but never war. There was nothing to fight over.

It was like motion-smoothing televisions vs. 24 fps; each camp felt extremely uncomfortable amongst the others. True, there could be various beings, human or otherwise, in either dimension 'switching sides', like the phenomenon of a white settler-girl kidnapped and raised by Native Americans, or vice versa, but it was rare.

Not to mention the extensive facilities and infrastructure required to even make inter-dimensional travel possible in the first place—the zipping mechanism, the 'Coat Check'. A being couldn't just wander freely, even, or they could, but it was extremely dangerous; extensive tools and training are required just to navigate.

A 2-D being would have no understanding of how space was oriented in 3D. The sense of sight and a "first-person" perspective are only possible in 3-D space, for example. It was extremely confusing to the uninitiated.

The pyramid elevator to the Navicenter hummed. Archive was going to make a Q-Call to the Pings. Everything Archive saw, heard, touched, tasted, or smelled was converted to data and permanently preserved on a computer within a computer within a computer, three levels down. The data was then spooned over and cross referenced with all previous data by his subconscious. His subconscious would inevitably have an opinion of its own. Which would float up the levels to a section of the Navicenter called POINT, and then be relayed to Archive.

But Archive was still formulating his own thoughts at the top level. And as always, time marched on. The hostages of the Dordent had water, but they were getting hungry. Attempts to deliver them food had resulted in failure.

Navicenter was beneath the base of the pyramid, which was a 4-point pyramid with a triangle base, and POINT was, obviously, at the top. The Pyramid itself was a ship, a clandestine offshoot of the Center for Interdimensional Travel, simply called TETRA.

The Pings were in 3-D space, which made communication easier. The call went through on a simple visual screen in front of Archive. On the other end was Noosh, one of the Ping ambassadors to TETRA. It had been several years since they had spoken, but Noosh remembered Archive, who tended to leave an impression. Archive, of course, also remembered Noosh.

"Archive. It's always a good day when I can see your ugly mug on my Com-Screen.

What's up?"

"Did you recently farm a Dordent purchased off King Lameer from Monze?"

"I don't know about recently, but yes. That was a while back, though. Oh, this is about the escape?"

"Yes."

"Oh god, what happened?"

"A section of a city on Earth was leveled."

"Oh no! On Earth? Archive, you have to understand that this whole thing was a mistake. A terrible accident."

Archive's subconscious was different than a normal human's. Whereas a human subconscious might keep deepest dreams and beliefs, as well as regulate things humans didn't think about like heartbeat and breathing, Archive's subconscious was off playing Sherlock Holmes by himself and reporting back via POINT.

The reports would come in the form of hunches. The process was still mysterious, even to him, but he had learned to trust it, trust his hunches, and even become superstitious about it. Now he blinked, and his subconscious delivered him a hunch.

"There will be an investigation, but I'm inclined to believe you. The question is what to do about it. It would help me if you told me what happened."

Noosh relayed the story:

The farming of the Dordent had been part of the deal with Monze. It was transferred to a Ping-controlled gravel quarry on a distant moon. This was a move from 2-D to 3-D, but the bagel-shaped laser-baking destruction had not happened by then. However, the roots were manifested from the beacon at that point, but the creature was peaceful.

The Pings built a gazing center to look at the Dordent for scientific research at first, but later the public was allowed, and the center became more of a zoo. "Come see a 2-D being!"

They quickly became aware of the Dordent's unzipped abilities that manifested when it was ripped from 2-D space. Keepers that got too close would get headaches, so nobody ventured within 150 feet, ever. One day, there was a murder: the sepholoric sac of a Ping was exploded, killing it instantly.

In response, the Pings hit back with an argon EMP, and the roots withered. The range of the psychotropic attacks waned, and infrastructure was built to prevent further destruction of observers and keepers.

The preventative measures were thus: one, a safety bubble of about 200 feet, and two, a permanent drain on the roots from the beacon. They had determined that the process of unzipping had continued through the roots, pulling out energy from the second dimension—a leak—and they could mine it. On a larger scale, energy leeching between dimensions like this could cause serious problems; war, or even destabilization. But at this scale, it was negligible. Even as a power plant, it wasn't viable on a larger scale. Yes, it produced energy that they could re-purpose and utilize, but not enough to make it worthwhile. It was, however, useful to keep the Dordent dormant.

Then one day, accelerationists sneaked in and sabotaged the safety measures of the Dordent containment. It's power quickly grew, like a power plant meltdown, and in the chaos to contain it, it had been warped away, back to the second dimension briefly, then quickly pulled back into the third dimension at a random safe distance, which unfortunately happened to be Earth. The double warp process was an emergency protocol. An investigation was held into whether or not the security team had jumped the gun. But because it had jumped twice, the Pings were unable to track it past the first jump, and it had escaped.

Like a world-class boxer with a pet tiger who'd escaped, the Pings waited nervously for reports, ready to help if necessary.

"Archive, if there's anything we can do…"

The problem was this: the technology that the Pings used to contain and harvest the energy of the Dordent would work on earth, but it was too far to transport, even using dimensional jumping. It would take too long to get the jump accurate, and the hostages would be dead. "Just cooperate with the ensuing investigations."

"Of course."

Archive was armed with blueprints, but no technology except what was available on Earth and Monze. But anything ripped from Monze would be affected by the change to 3-D and couldn't be relied on.

He had a theory: that the creature could see and was using sight above all else for spatial reasoning, and as it was originally a two-dimensional being, it didn't understand the spatial organization of our sense of sight in the 3-D realm.

From its time in captivity, it had manifested a hatred for its captors, the Pings, who, from their silhouette far away, would be read as humans. But it was only exposed to them at great distances because of the safety barrier, so they appeared "small" to it, rather than "far away."

The Dordent hated all small humanoid beings, if they were larger, it would cease to hate them; The Dordent would distinguish them as something different, something it didn't hate. To grow bigger in the eyes of the Dordent, all one had to do was get closer to it.

This theory mapped over the donut-shaped destruction well. Those close to the Dordent were spared, as they were seen as large beings. While further away, everything was destroyed, until it passed out of range of what the Dordent identified as a Ping captor or could see at all.

Lastly, the distance of the safety barrier at the Ping compound mapped almost exactly over the destruction in the city on earth. So the trick was, how to pass through the donut?

Archive had been in communication with a liaison on Earth, the captain of the primary response team, a man familiar with the workings of TETRA, and they had been running some experiments.

They tried sending crash-test dummies in. The Dordent left them alone. Similarly, birds were observed to be unaffected. It seemed it would only attack living humanoid beings. They thought they could send a drone in and communicate, but the energy field emitting from the Dordent's beacon was shutting down all electronics. And even if they could speak with it, there would still be the problem of getting through the donut danger zone to reach the hostages. And even if they managed to reach the hostages, there was still the problem of getting them out.

The first human hadn't been sent yet; it was too much of a risk. The response team constructed special dummies to simulate human body-temperatures. Complete with little pump heaters and sacs of warm water in their chest, and carbon dioxide emitters from the mouth orifice. They drove a car remotely, with the warmed dummy in the driver's seat, and entered the donut zone at 20 miles per hour. The dummy's chest was exploding 50 feet into the donut-zone. Interesting, but also unfortunate. Apparently, the Dordent could sense heat.

They tried another car at 160 miles per hour. Would speed make travel through the donut safer? Sadly, no. That dummy's chest was exploding as well.

They tested blind spots, approached from directly above it with a drone, and warmed a dummy. The chest exploded.

What about beneath? Then send a dummy in through the sewer. The chest exploded.

They tried packing a warm dummy on ice. Exploded. But the dummy made it 100 feet, instead of just fifty, into the donut zone.

A back-and-forth discussion with the Dordent was impossible, but they were testing one-way communications, visuals, white flags, as well as calming music blasted from outside the energy field and messages of peace. Might as well. However, there was no response.

It was thought that maybe someone already in the core of the donut, one of the hostages, would be able to talk to it and act as an intermediary if they could blast orders loud enough from outside the donut. But again, there was no good way for a hero-hostage to get back to them.

They had tried to drop food, water, and some weapons on the roof twice so far, but the first time, the wind had blown the crate to the east and it had missed the drop. The second time, the crate had landed on the beacon of the Dordent itself on its way down, and at that point had exploded.

While Archive suspected the Dordent had something akin to the sense of sight that allowed it to map out the space around it, he had no idea about any other senses—sound, touch, etc. All these things act in different ways and serve different purposes in 2-D and 3-D space. It wasn't likely the Dordent had organs that could "hear" in the way humans can. Beyond that, there was just the simple issue of a language barrier. So, they were waiting for Archive.

Archive had collected quite a bit of useful info on the Dordent. The Pings claimed there was no evidence that the Dordent could see. They had scans of it along multiple vectors of measurement. He knew exactly what it looked like, inside and out. It's true, the "beacon"

technically wasn't an eye, but it was functioning like one in 3-D space; something was allowing it to identify the beings around it, and kill them if they were too small.

In 2-Dimensional space, senses that pick up the information of bouncing waves (light and sound) were relatively useless. Instead, special feelers were called "Tendra." Tendra were like millions of invisible ropes constantly scanning the creature's surroundings.

With Tendra, everything was the same "size" at any distance, but the distance between beings was still measured, which was valuable. The Dordent had Tendra, like all 2-Dimensional beings. But Tendra were immeasurable in 3-D space. With Tendra, the thought was that the Dordent should have been able to accept all human beings as relatively the same size. It should have been "feeling" them. Could there be a way that the feelers scanned far-away people as small and closer people as large?

It depended on how the information was translated by the Dordent's brain. Scanning with eyes, near and far in 3-D space, scanning with feelers, near and far in 3-D space, or even radar—it was the same information that came in. But because it was a 2-D to 3-D brain that was translating it, something was getting lost in translation. And the Dordent did have a brain. The Pings had confirmed that. Like holding a chess piece in one palm, one close to the chest, and the other arm being 100 feet long, stretched out; also holding a chess piece. How would the mind's eye picture the pieces side by side?

In any case, the Dordent was acting on a previously created prejudice: that the chess piece held in the long arm was its hated captor, and the piece held close was something different and non-threatening.

Understanding the Dordent's physiology could help understand its motives, which could help the negotiation process, should one arrive. But the more important problem still existed: how to even reach it in the first place.

The first plan was advanced: to cut off the field, to "blind" it. To do this, they would drop a giant tarp on the entire building. The hostages would no doubt be alarmed, so new messages were blasted down the causeway toward the Nakatomi building. "A tarp will cover the windows, do not be alarmed."

The tarp was manifested in the 2-D space above the building and fell. 2-D space couldn't handle many shapes, but a tarp most certainly could. King Griswold was happy to accommodate, in accordance with the investigation, as his kingdom was close enough within the inter-dimensional miasma to make it possible in the first place.

The responding forces of the city, as well as countless civilians outside the danger zone of the donut, looked up as a giant black square was manifested in the sky above the Nakatomi Building and fell.

Like putting a caged bird to sleep, Archive thought. He was skeptical it would work, as the Pings had never employed such a tactic with the Dordent, but he needed to start with something simple compared to the other possible plans.

The huge tarp fell; no one was close enough to touch it, but if they could've, they wouldn't have believed it. Royal fabric from 2-D space! Pure black, light as a feather. The Dordent could seemingly see through the streets to the sewers. It could see through tinted glass. It saw all in the danger zone of the donut. What about 2-D fabric? The gesture itself could open new avenues. Time would tell.

But with a tarp that large, it was hard to imagine or even run a simulation of how it would fall. Nobody had seen anything like that before, but it fell very evenly.

Because it was so large, the vast majority of the remaining cloth mass pulled tight any section that was making noise or warping. All in all, it was four square miles, two by two. It blocked out most of the sky completely for anyone who stood in the danger zone of the donut, but everyone in that zone had already died. Further out, it was far enough away to allow for dispassionate observation.

The tarp fell and folded, with the fulcrum of all folds at the head of the Dordent. Now all there was to see was a giant spire of black cloth in the middle of the city, with death all around it.

Archive didn't anticipate that the visual would be so striking. *Now we test it*, he thought.

Another dummy was sent in.

"How fast?" The programmer of the remote car wanted to know.

"Go slow, two miles per hour," Archive said. They hadn't yet tested a super-slow approach. He laughed to himself; his younger self would chastise him for not controlling variables. Say the approach *did* work; they wouldn't know if it was because of the slow-moving car or the tarp!

The car ventured forth slowly. And they waited. They could hear their own breath and the wind above them. The remote car slowly rolled towards the huge black spire in the city. Could it work? Archive was already planning the next option. He didn't have a good feeling about this one.

But the car made it further than the other cars and dummies had. The programmer on the console watched as the visual feed grew fuzzy. There was definitely some kind of field out there surrounding the Dordent.

They switched to analog sniper scopes. Archive took one himself and perched from a good viewpoint. *Been awhile*, he thought. He watched as the dummy's chest exploded. It had made it about halfway through the danger zone of the donut: 300 feet.

"Well, Archive, what now?" The captain asked, pinching his cigar tighter than usual. "So the tarp didn't work; how do we get it off?"

Archive smiled. "We can't."

"It can see through everything, like we're all naked."

Archive clarified the captain's statement to himself: "It scans us, and the information is filtered to a mental vision that an eye in 3-D space would see, but there's no eye."

"Maybe we just can't see the eye."

"Exactly!" Archive handed his sniper rifle to one of the responders and started pacing with his hands behind his back.

The captain put his cigar back in his mouth and waited.

Archive turned and looked at him. "Next test," he said.

They had allowed civilian observers to linger at a safe distance up until this point. But now Archive's test required top secret military technology to be utilized, and the area was further cleared, with barriers set up extending the diameter of the affected zone by an extra mile.

Civilian observers noted the zest with which the military jumped into action to guard the new borders. It appeared to overshadow the actual rescue response to the Dordent in the first place, which, in fairness, was being run by a small team at TETRA with little desire for power-play optics.

The technology in question was the second Star Satellite, still under construction. The first was already secretly in orbit. The Star Satellite acted like a bully burning ants through a magnifying glass. The giant magnifying glass was in orbit to focus the sun's rays into a laser.

Archive had to explain his plan before the captain understood that they weren't going to burn the Dordent with a giant laser, as that would endanger the hostages. They didn't need the Star Satellite's burning capability at all; what they needed was the giant magnifying glass.

One was already up in orbit, but the other was still in the factory in Alabama. As usual, Archive's subconscious had suggested he get the ball moving with this even before it would be required. So he'd sent for it right away. It had been transported via airdrop and was already nearby.

His subconscious warned him again—one more thing. The Star Satellite Polymer Magnifying Glass would need to be used in more than one experiment.

Does that mean this one will fail? Archive thought back.

Another message: a gut feeling translated by Archive's conscious brain as his own thought. *There's no such thing as a failed experiment.*

Shut up, Archive thought.

At this point, the hostages had been in darkness for 48 hours, and it was unclear how much water or food they had. Some of the early attempts at communication were to impart to them the importance of staying put and how dangerous it was to venture into the donut. Beyond dangerous, because just "danger" implied they might survive. They would die if they stepped into the donut zone; the Dordent would scan them as a 'small being,' register their BTUs, and explode their chest.

Whether or not they had heeded these warnings or learned in fateful ways would be discovered only if Archive ever managed to reach them. He had to decide with each test whether it was worth risking his own life. This plan was promising; the giant magnifying glass would be used to enlarge the Dordent's readings of humans in the donut zone, hopefully rendering them safe.

The magnifying glass was about 300 feet wide, therefore another problem arose: it was too big. It couldn't fit between the buildings in the street approaching the Nakatomi Building, where the Dordent had taken root. They could fly it in with helicopters; that's how they had gotten it from Alabama, but surrounding skyscrapers made it extremely technical to get it in place.

The weight distribution and the new angle of the giant polymer that were needed made it too dangerous. They didn't have pilot-less helicopters for the heavy-lifter Chinook models yet. And they didn't want any pilots having their chests exploded by the Dordent or crashing from the EMP energy field. They would have to do it 'analog' if they did it at all. It was also heavy and almost impossible to move. The captain told Archive as much, but now he was losing his patience and was ready to start risking human lives if they had to.

"Captain," Archive said, "I'm disappointed in you; can't you see?"

"What?"

"Look at it!" Archive said.

The captain looked at the giant magnifying glass laid out on the field of the HQ they had set up in the central park of the city. It took four trucks with platforms to move it around in this open space, all moving in unison. Heavy-lifting helicopters had flown in and dropped it. It was huge and heavy, and he could only see it from the side, like a coin on a table at that angle.

"What, Archive? Spit it out!"

"It's circular," Archive said.

"So?"

"So... we roll it." There was a large street opening, a big intersection, in front of the Nakatomi building, with enough space that the magnifying glass could be rotated at that point to be perpendicular to the street approaching the building. Cables would be used at that point to rotate it from outside the donut zone.

Unfortunately, this meant the magnifying glass, which was actually made of a special polymer, could only be used in one 'experiment.' Then it would be in place until the situation was resolved, just like the giant tarp.

Lastly, the polymer would have to be lifted. However, because it would already be in the correct position, the safety cables, extending outside of the Dordent's donut zone, would be used to reel in several giant helium balloons. This alone wouldn't be enough, but now the Chinook helicopters could be used once again, this time just two, with the helium working in conjunction to balance the polymer upright, and allowing for the cables to be long enough to create a good safety margin for the Chinook helicopters outside of the donut zone, which they had discovered extended upwards as well.

The eye saw in all directions, making it more of a thick dome than a donut. But the term 'donut' had already caught on amongst the response team. Even Archive preferred it.

All this played out smoothly, and the tests began. Slow, fast, cold, hot...

Can we see what the Dordent sees? Archive thought. They had a helicopter fly around from the reverse angle behind the Dordent's beacon and snap some footage with a super-zoom lens through the magnifying polymer to the street.

They had to admit, it was working as a function of making the dummies look bigger. And they were getting farther than they ever had before. The donut run had to be 600 feet, and the previous farthest was only 200 feet- not even halfway. These dummies made it 400 feet before their chests exploded.

"Well, it's progress," the captain lamented.

Archive was distracted; he snapped out of it and said, "We have another problem."

"What is it this time!?"

Archive faced the Captain while pointing down the street away from the Nakatomi building and the Dordent, "The sun is setting; it's gonna move behind the magnifying glass soon and fry all the hostages." They would have to move the giant polymer away and save any further tests in that thread for tomorrow.

They had time for one more attempt for the day. It was an opportunity to implement Archive's third and final plan. But the third plan could not be re-tested easily. Archive's subconscious delivered him inspiration for a decision: This would be, for him, a real and final attempt.

Archive's last idea was to be implemented, The Humanoid Float. A giant would approach, one big enough for the Dordent to register it as a large being, even from 600 feet away. Archive would stow away in a compartment in the lower-gut, in the fetal position, hoping to make any silhouette he might strike with his heat register just as a ball rather than a threatening small humanoid shape.

The Giant would be heated with air pumps to match Archive's own body temperature. If it was cold, the Dordent would see through Archive's illusion easily, but if it were heated, it would mask Archive's BTU signature, and he would appear as an organ to a larger, non-threatening being.

Finally, the placement of Archive's chamber had been chosen carefully to be just outside of the chest and ribcage area that the Dordent had been typically choosing to explode in its victims. Hypothetically, this meant that even if the plan didn't work, Archive could survive at least the first explosion.

He would still be smack-dab in the donut zone, and in this hypothetical situation, he would be relying on his subconscious. To this thought, his subconscious delivered him an instantaneous deduction: *I don't recommend you rely on me in that scenario.*

There was a Macy's Day Parade float that had been constructed twenty years ago but was never used because it was too big. It worked fine; even to this day, it was just too expensive to keep the air pumps running all throughout it for an entire parade, so it had remained in storage. It was a giant tiger- Hobbes, from the old comic book series, *Calvin and Hobbes.*

The creator, Bill Waterson, had famously lamented any merchandising of his iconic comic and never gave permission; the Hobbes float was never used, which spared him extra grief should he ever find out, but now it was about to be the final attempt to save 200 people.

Hobbes had been 'on deck' for the previous 24 hours. The response team had spent this time augmenting his shape somewhat to make him look even more naturally humanoid. Archive had deliberated somewhat over this point. The problem was that Hobbes actually looked stunningly similar to a Ping. Humans in the donut zone were being seemingly mistaken for Pings as it was, but if you scaled them up, the differences in the silhouette became more obvious.

No matter how big a Ping appeared, it would explode, with the Dordent openly sparing people inside the safety zone. The augmentations included shortening Hobbes' arms, cutting up his crotch to make his legs longer, and binding his nose. The resulting creature was an abomination, but nonetheless humanoid. Archive was nervous about this but reminded himself that the Hobbes float was an abomination even before all the augmentation, and the silhouette was what was really important.

He'd felt the stakes rising himself—all the work, the experiments—and with every test, they had grown closer to beating it, but would this be the final test, for him at least, one way or the other. It was a battle of wits against a god. And he was about to risk his life.

They closed the chamber and gave him a little bottle of warm water. Archive started the timer in his head. Even he wouldn't be able to last long in the heart chamber, and multiple actions had to be carefully synchronized. Archive had opted out of keeping some communications in the heart chamber with him. *They stop working anyway*, he thought. *This will either work, or it won't.*

The giant, augmented Hobbes took its first step.

There were some things he did keep in a container beneath the lower-gut chamber: a chainsaw, pliers, a shotgun, some dynamite, and beneath that, some water and snacks for the hostages.

The Captain watched from the console in the park. "300 feet. Halfway."

A spotter ventured a response, "Promising."

"It's always promising- until it's not," the Captain lamented.

Archive thought about what he might find. Would the hostages be okay? It wasn't clear if they were affected by the Dordent in some way too. It could be cancer years from now. Or something more immediate, something worse.

They could all be zombies, Archive thought. That's why he'd brought the shotgun.

"500 feet." They were officially the farthest they'd ever been.

The magnifying glass was still in place, creating a Matryoshka nesting doll effect. At first, the Hobbes float would be magnified; finally, as it got closer, it would pass out of the ring that was magnified by the polymer, but its chest would still be magnified. Like a monster shedding its skin as it approached, it would change shapes and iterations depending on the magnification and perspective, but at any point, it was large enough to not have its chest explode.

The tarp might have been having some effect as well; it did seem to allow the warmed dummies to pass a little further into the donut zone.

Hobbes took the last step. "600 feet!"

"Now what?" They were all looking at the Black Spire, with the magnifying glass, and the Hobbes Abomination. There was still a clear problem: the Hobbes Abomination didn't reach high enough—not even close. The top of Hobbes was a little less than halfway up the building.

"Now we watch and wait," the Captain said.

Archive had one item on his naked body, an analog stopwatch, which only served to confirm the time he was keeping in his head: It was almost time. He had reached the distance horizontally, but was technically still beneath the safety zone.

He felt the head of the Hobbes Giant bump against the polymer; beyond that, just 20 or 30 feet, was the building, cloaked in 2-D cloth. The final and most important augmentation to the Hobbes Abomination was now utilized. Hobbes had several hooks beneath his upper lip, meant to catch the rim of the huge polymer magnifier. Spotters relayed between the ground and the helicopters; it was a precise movement, but they didn't have to get it on the first try. However, luckily, they did. Archive felt the Hobbes lifting, now hanging, his two 'fangs' cinched fast to the rim of the polymer.

Observers from outside the donut zone, and even some civilians who had found good perches upon which to get a view, witnessed as the Hobbes abomination was raised up the spire toward the beacon.

He waited. He felt Hobbes move again—some shuffling.

Then... stop.

It was time. If his calculations were correct, the Hobbes Abomination should be looking at a sheet of black 2-Dimensional cloth. Beyond which would be the 24th and 25th floors of the Nakatomi building, the core of the safety zone from the Dordent's wrath, and the inner donut hole. This would mean he was in the safety zone. He had made it! How he would get back was another question.

Here goes nothing, he thought.

He opened the chamber; damn, it was hot in there! He grabbed his stuff and moved to the catwalk to the outer rim of the Hobbes Abomination's lower gut. He made an incision. *Sorry, Hobbes*, he thought.

Then he was looking at the 2-D black cloth. It was so dark that it looked like he could fall into it. He had to fight a sense of vertigo. He logged a small piece of data: how 2-D cloth behaves in 3-D when being cut. It was so smooth and light that it would slip off the knife; he had to puncture it first, then cut.

Then he saw them—the hostages—gathered, staring at him from behind a huge window. "Stand back!" He yelled.

Archive had to make a choice. He had found the Dordent's heart in a janitor's closet; it was reinforced with a huge clamshell-type material, but there was one survivor who had offered to help pry it open, and Archive could get the chainsaw in there if he had to.

The only problem was that the Dordent in its death throes, could explode all their chests. The other option was to talk to it. But he had thus far failed to do so. He'd tried 500 languages. The problem was that he didn't know where its ear was. It was like talking to a tree. It was embarrassing. He asked everyone to leave the room so he could have some privacy.

The polymer lens had been flown away, and the hostages had food. They had time now. Enough time to get the Ping technology to handle this scenario peacefully? Archive considered this. The Dordent was a godlike being, after all. It would be a shame to kill it.

The Captain knew Archive had time, so he was patient. The sun had already set. They were reorganizing the response team; only a few would stay overnight. The Captain had volunteered. He was still curious.

At 0300 that night, he was presented with a paper airplane that had been spotted flying through the donut zone and landed in the park about 150 feet away. He knew immediately it was from Archive, who would have gotten a kick out of the analog communication technique. One of the only times it would actually be useful and not self-indulgent. Not too self-indulgent, at least.

He unwrapped the paper airplane and confirmed his suspicions. Archive had written it and let it fly into the night sky towards the captain. They were so high up that the paper airplane was able to cross a great distance in the windless night, through the donut zone, all the way to the captain.

Archive related his plan to open communications with the Pings to resolve the scenario peacefully. It would take two weeks. They would have to completely ration the food Archive had brought, but it would work.

But there was a problem: the donut zone was sprinkled with over two thousand human corpses with exploded chests. It had already been several days; they were starting to rot. Rats and seagulls had begun feasting; that alone was an issue to keep an eye on. The donut zone was uninhabitable in the meantime, but the pungent stench of a rotting battlefield was an ever-evolving variable. It'd be best if they could clean it up. The good news was that rib cages make easy targets for hooked lines and other useful cleanup tools.

Bags of lye were slingshot in to hit the dead bodies. The sewers were temporarily sealed up just past the Nakatomi building, causing the area in front to spill over into the streets. It was just a blanket wash, but it was useful in conjunction with the lye.

Finally, giant hooked nets were dropped and dragged across and out of the donut zone, picking up dead bodies as they went. If they caught on to anything too resilient, that section of the net could be cut open with an incision from a laser sniper. Bodies deep inside city structures would be harder or impossible to exhume, but it was a start. Then there was the arduous process of identifying the bodies and notifying the next of kin. Thus, the time passed with these great projects and undertakings.

And so it happened; eight days into the two-week wait for the Pings, Archive managed to open communications with the Dordent.

There was a particularly airy vent in the men's bathroom on the 24th floor that Archive was able to interface with. Record keepers for Monze had deduced a language that the Dordent would finally respond to, like whale-speak, but instead of being higher than humans could hear, it had a lower register.

They had also found the central nervous trunk of the brain. They could bomb it and, in theory, safely eliminate any possibility of retaliation from the Dordent. Much like how an elite cop might shoot the medulla oblongata of a perp to stop their finger from twitching.

"Dordent? Greetings and good day."

"You know my language?"

Archive gave a pause for effect, then responded, "I do."

"Speak, Medium-Cage, what would you like to say to me? It tickles me that a little being like you might have a conversation with a godly genius like me."

Archive noticed the Dordent was calling him "Medium-Cage." His subconscious delivered an instantaneous deduction: Small-Cages were what the Dordent hated and exploded. Medium and Large Cages were spared.

"They call you a Dordent; did you know that?"

"Why wouldn't I?"

"Do you like that name?"

The Dordent rumbled, "Beings aren't meant to name themselves; I don't sit here looking in the mirror all day. Truth be told, I'm not crazy about it. But that's the least of my problems right now."

"What problem do you prioritize?"

"These damn Pings, that's what," the Dordent said. "They keep me captive and won't let me go; they keep me weak, at only a fraction of my godly powers. My intellect is all I have. I thought I'd escaped, but now there's just more of them. Damn things followed me somehow."

Archive gave another pause, "Yes…"

"But I killed them all. I can't stand the Pings. They kept me captive for years. At least now I am free, but I'm stuck here."

"And you're not angry with the creatures near your vicinity now, like me?"

"No, no, you people didn't do anything to me. I am a fair and just god. Except I saw a few people shrink and turn into Pings, so I killed them. Shapeshifters are fine with me, by all accounts, but shapeshifting into a loathsome Ping, I can't abide."

Archive hesitated to explain the situation truthfully. There was still a risk that the Dordent could murder them all. But he had confirmed his hypothesis and was glad.

"Dordent, can I have a special heart-to-heart conversation with you? But not yet—in a few days. I'm going to try and get you out of here, take you anywhere you want to go, and then we can talk."

"Why not just talk now? We are here."

"I want to free you first, then talk."

"Where would I want to go?"

"You tell me. Just somewhere safe, for you and all other creatures, even Pings."

"Pings! If I see any, I'll kill them."

Archive considered his response. His subconscious gave him a hint of where this was going, and he prepared the coming line: "Well, we can just keep you and them separate, avoid further conflict; that would be good for everyone."

"Are you on their side?"

"No, if anything, I'm on your side; I'm trying to free you."

"If you free me, I vow to wage war on all Pings for eternity."

"An eye for an eye, is that it?"

"Exactly."

Archive thought. The line his subconscious had hinted at had appeared. He could launch a different gambit now, separate from the truth gambit, but it would have to be now. Unfortunately, it wouldn't work to try it at a later date. He could wait until later and stick with the truth gambit, but that would just be kicking the can down the road. Or he could ax the central nervous system now, which in itself was just another dangerous gambit.

"Medium-Cage?" the Dordent questioned.

Archive gave his response. "Well, you've already killed 6 thousand Pings; every Ping who ever wronged you is dead."

"That so? Serves those bastards right. I did, didn't I? I exploded them. That'll show them."

"Would you be willing to spare any further Ping bloodshed? As the remaining generations, of which there are only a few, didn't do anything to you and had nothing to do with your capture and imprisonment? After all, the war is won. If you continue a war after winning, that's just genocide at that point, and you are a just god."

"Maybe genocide is what I want after what they've done."

"You'll have freedom; you can do anything, and you've won. Why would you drag yourself back into a conflict after that? Justice has already been done; you will be free."

Archive waited; no response. He rose and started to leave.

"Medium Cage…"

"Yes?"

"Let me think about it."

Archive praised the heavens, saying that he did have time to spare for the Dordent to mull things over. And, as fate would have it, the Dordent did. Over the next few days and a few more conversations, it became pacified regarding the prospects of bloody revenge against the Pings.

But there was a problem, of course: this whole resolution was contingent on the falsehood that it was Pings the Dordent had killed and not humans. The Dordent still didn't understand how 3-D space was organized compared to 2-D space. Archive had planned on telling it, but now he couldn't.

The Dordent would be returned to 2-D space in a realm where it could do no harm and be free. The Pings were ordered to steer clear of it and agreed to this.

This whole time, Archive had to stay within the donut hole safety zone until the final warp was ready, ironically done with Ping technology. The hostages were left behind, but Archive agreed to go with the Dordent upon its request.

The Ping technology, a series of tubes and levers, was installed and charged. Archive was given a corresponding wristwatch to aid in his return, paired with the mother charge from ground zero on the top floors of the Nakatomi building.

Archive had checked and double-checked to make sure the Dordent would not be triggered into a violent response by the sudden appearance of Ping technology. He had been assured the Dordent would have no way of identifying it, but it still felt like a risk.

As actual Pings could not help in the installation, Archive had been given an extremely detailed book of instructions that he read in .05 of a second, and he was able to warp in a human team from TETRA at that close range. Everything had gone smoothly. Archive fought back the part of himself that was overly aware of superstition. It's always dangerous when things go too smoothly.

The installation was charged, and Archive asked the Dordent if it was ready to warp. Upon confirmation, he activated the drive on his wrist, FOOM.

They were in 2-D Space now, so their sight had reverted to more of a laser-guided "feeling." It was disorienting for Archive, even with the headset to help him organize the sensory information in this dimension.

The Dordent spoke. "You said you would have a special conversation with me when I was free. Well, now I'm free, Medium-Cage. What did you want to say to me?"

Damn, Archive thought. *What should I even pretend that I want to say?* "Why do you call me Medium-Cage, Dordent?"

"In this world, there are Extra-Large-Cages, like the one they put me in. Big-Cages, like my branches, for the lightning birds; Medium-Cages, like you; and Tiny-Cages, like the Pings, which I explode."

"Ah."

"Is that all you wanted to ask? This is your one chance to talk to a godly genius. I can reveal the secrets of this universe, or others, to you. I can offer you untold wisdom—the secret of life. All you have to do is ask, Medium-Cage."

Archive readied his warp to his own freedom, back in 3-D space. He couldn't decide if he was feeling affection or annoyance in that moment. "No," he said. "No, thank you."

"But, Medium-Cage, surely you would want to pick my brain about something. It's not every day you get such a chance as to talk to the likes of me."

With the warp ready, Archive thought to himself, *Why not?* He turned to the Dordent, with his thumb on the drive button. "Ignorance is bliss. Goodbye, Dordent."

He bowed, then he warped out of there, leaving the Dordent floating in space.

The Dordent floated for a good while, then thought to itself. *The irony that a humble Medium-Cage would deliver to me a nugget of advice that so many throughout the universe find useful. Ignorance is bliss. Yes, it certainly is. Medium-Cage, it is. Wisdom can be found in the most unexpected of places, even from a mere mortal Medium-Cage. Sadly, such advice would never apply to me. I'm doomed to know all, and suffer the consequences, for all eternity.*

BUGGED

BY WILLIAM PERDOMO

"It's a new day, and every new day is a chance for a new beginning." That was the mantra Stephen repeated to himself whenever he got that familiar rise in his pulse and that tingle at the back of his neck, like the weight of all his problems, known and unknown, were tugging at him for solutions to every one of them at the same time. He often compared the feeling to a funnel, where the universe pours in all its challenges simultaneously, only to remain trapped in the sticky fear centers of his brain, unaddressed.

See, it's happening again, he thought, with his eyes shut tight to reality. *Now, say the words, 'today is a new day.'* Immediately he felt that his most stressful imaginary life had vanished as the mind spell rode the utterance through the perfect seventy-five degree air, answered by a gentle off-shore Los Angeles breeze. *For now,* he told himself; forever the pessimist.

"One problem at a time. Don't let them stack! Problem one: apartment." He gazed down at the local rag he was holding tightly between his fingers. Stephen hadn't noticed that he'd crumbled and ripped it during his brief disassociation. "How long have I been standing here?" He said this to himself as he began to grow self-conscious about the possibility that every passerby thought he was a schizoid loser, which he knew he was but hoped no one else could suss out by looking at him.

"Fuck," he barked, "stop doing that!" After shaking his head, then drawing and exhaling a deep breath, Stephen was back to the task at hand. Back to the present, where he realized he was still standing on the sidewalk at the base of a driveway and still speaking out loud, which had stopped a teenage girl from walking her dog. Stephen looked to his left up the driveway and then back at the teenager standing in the street, who was still staring at him along with her yapping chihuahua. He darted his eyes from side to side and cracked an awkward smile, unsure of how to wiggle out of such a vulnerable situation. She smiled sympathetically but kept her half-closed eyes on him, studying him like a bored child would a squirrel she had seen fall from the fence a thousand times.

"Did I just say all that out loud?" He asked, knowing the answer.

"Yes, you did," she replied in a flat tone under already bored eyes.

"Even the 'fuck'?"

"Even the 'fuck.'"

"I'm not from around here."

There was a long pause before she answered. "You'll fit in just fine." With that, she disappeared down the road, her dog yapping and her Chuck Taylors crunching on the asphalt.

The ad in the paper led him up a long driveway that wound back in on itself around a dried-up fountain decorated in blue and white tiles. Beyond that, detached apartments surrounded the entrance to a court yard. All of them were small, single-story bungalows that were cheap and cozy enough for his needs.

Stephen was checking the listing again to make sure he was headed in the right direction towards the manager's unit when shattering glass and screaming snapped him out of the tentative calm he had achieved on his short walk from the street on up to where he was now. *Did I just hear that? Or was it anxiety?* He stopped and listened, his mind slamming towards and between possible explanations, all concluding that he could be hallucinating, and, *Why not? It's happened before. I took my pill, right? Yeah, one this morning.* So it was impossible that he was having an episode. That is, if the medicine was still effective. His pulse rose a bit at the thought, but Stephen told himself to trust his therapist- and her prescriptions.

He had just regained his calm when out of the bungalow in front of him stumbled a man in a yellow jump suit, muck boots, and blood squishing through fingers pressed tightly to a cut on his scalp. He was groaning and smearing red across his face. Stephen froze and doubted his reality again. His eyes snapped wide at the same time as his heart leapt into his throat when the man saw him and threw his weight forward on shaky legs, which gave out, making him fall into a reluctant catch. Stephen held onto him as he slid down to his waist, staining his pressed button-up shirt *with blood tainted with God knows what!*

The revulsion at the thought hadn't had time to make its way through the funnel when more crashing and yelling distracted Stephen from dwelling on fear and insecurity. Rather, a morbid curiosity seized him and drew him towards where the man had emerged. "Stay here," he said, leaving the man laying on his side in the courtyard. The man propped himself up on one elbow and yelled after him, "The fuck, dude, I might have a cracked skull. Call the cops!"

Approaching the open door out of which the wounded man had escaped, Stephen pressed himself flat against the stucco wall and slid along it until he could quickly peek around the door for a second before reflexively snapping his head back into cover as a glass object exploded right where his face had been. "Who was *that* fucker?" Screeched a male voice followed by a calmer, almost amused female reply, "Probably a cop, you fucking psycho! The whole neighborhood can hear you." Her voice doubled in amplitude. "Billy, are you okay?"

Stephen was about to answer on behalf of the injured man, now named Billy, when the male with the annoying high-pitched voice cut in, "*Fuck* Billy! He was trying to kill my *babies*, and you were going to let him, you bitch!"

"They're just *bugs*, you whacko! Last warning, Arnie: Get the hell out or I'm calling the cops," she delivered in a lower but stern voice on the verge of giggling. From inside cover, Stephen thought he had enough to go on that this, in all likelihood, was actually happening, which was comforting enough to move him to a solution by asking, "Hey, lady, are you all right in there?"

She shot back, "You can hear the crazy midget yelling and breaking stuff, right? So that's a pretty stupid question."

Arnie nearly cut her off by piping up with that irritating squealing, "Get lost; jerk off. This is between me and this cunt!"

"Hey, Prince Valiant, I could use a hand in here." She asked, ignoring the nasty pejorative with the grace of someone who had heard it many times before.

Right, Stephen said to himself.

He pushed away from the wall, raised his hands, and then stepped through the doorway. What he saw nearly made him involuntarily chuckle and doubt, yet again, if he was indeed seeing things. Arnie's frame was exactly as Stephen had pictured it when he first heard that rat-like squeal out in the courtyard. Short, hunched, and thin, Arnie had a long neck beneath an unusually blocky head, topped with faded blue, greasy hair. In each hand, he was holding porcelain plates that made him look like a monkey about to bash together symbols.

Standing opposite him was a woman a good head taller, her hands balled into fists resting on her hips. Her hair was long, jet black, and separated across the forehead by blunt bangs above a round, pale face with rings through both sides of her bottom lip. The black shirt and jeans she wore were tight around a curvy figure that Stephen's eyes leered over before Arnie's slightly askew jaw wagged an accusation his way.

"So, this is the guy you replaced *me* with? First you gas all my babies, then you take my queen hostage; now you bring another guy into my place."

"*Your* place?" She chortled, "This was and is *my* house, you little blue-haired gremlin. And your 'babies' are fucking insects! Now, give me what you owe me, and I'll hand over your little girlfriend."

Feeling like the third man in a Mexican stand-off, Stephen took a few steps over broken plate shards, crunching them into the hardwood floor with a loud crack. He held one finger up like a kid, asking the teacher for attention, "Look, guys." Both of them snapped their heads in his direction. "I have no idea what I've walked into, but I've never met either of you. I'm just here about the ap—"

"Shut up. He doesn't care what you say. He's going to assume we're fucking." Arnie's mouth dropped a bit as he looked at the woman, then right back at Stephen with his beady little eyes narrowed and his plates slightly raised. Her bluntness shocked Stephen, and her indelicacy put him on edge, knowing that this little guy was unstable and ready to spring on either of them. "But we're not," he blurted out before looking Arnie in the eye with all sincerity and pleading, "we're not!"

Looking at the ceiling in disinterested exasperation and shaking her head, the woman scoffed, "Just shut up, dude, and try and look threatening. That's all this little prick understands." Arnie jerked his thin arm at the woman and launched a plate, which she easily dodged by leaning slightly to the side. It whistled past and broke to pieces against the wall behind her, leaving a dent in the drywall. "You think that guy is going to boot me out of my own house!"

"That's another fix you're going to owe me for, and from the looks of him, it's going to be a combination of the two of us."

"Look, lady, I can hold my own," Stephen added.

Stephen's interruption raised Arnie's temper enough to draw his ire and fixate on him as his perceived rival. He advanced towards the interloper, ready to pounce. Arnie jabbed at the air, his hand still gripping the plate, as the irritating voice resonated within his small body, causing his fury to intensify. "You think you can take me, pretty boy?" He squirted out from between clenched teeth and a spray of saliva.

The woman laughed, "I think he can." Stephen was confused. Did this lady want to calm the situation or not? "Wait, stop instigating," he blurted out while Arnie continued to move closer.

A small war cry issued out of Arnie's pencil neck, which startled Stephen, followed by him screaming, "We'll see about that!" He threw the last remaining plate at Stephen, which he narrowly dodged by ducking underneath it. By the time he was back up, Arnie was right on top of him, his gangly arms raised, and his thin fingers about to dig into Stephen's face. Before he could complete his attack, a broom handle broke across the back of Arnie's skull, which knocked him out cold at Stephen's feet.

The woman held up the broken shaft, flashing a smile around her straight white teeth, while the latter stood frozen, still wondering what the hell had just happened. "Whew," she laughed, "thanks." She tossed the broken piece of wood next to Arnie's face, around which a pool of saliva had already formed, then grabbed Stephen's hand and shook it. "What's your name?"

"St-Stephen."

"Thanks, Stevo. You were the perfect distraction. Did you see Billy out there?"

"I—I don't know. He looked hurt," he said, still shaking her hand.

The woman shouted past Stephen's head, which made him wince and take back his hand to protect his hearing. "Billy, are you okay?" The reply drifted back from the courtyard, "Yeah, I guess." The woman dismissed Billy with a wave of her hand. "He's fine," she said, then looked down at Arnie, still knocked out between them. The woman kicked him hard in the ribs and yelled, "That's for calling me a cunt!"

Finally, those eyes settled on Stephen. "I'm Mia."

Like a seething lab rat staring out his enclosure, Arnie bore daggers into Mia and Stephen standing on the curb from the back of a LAPD black and white. Mia met those crazy lamps head-on over the shoulder of the police officer, who was jotting down her statement on a notepad. She crossed her eyes, bent her head to one side, and stuck out her tongue at her former lover.

"All right, ma'am, I think we have all we need." As the officer raised his head, Mia instantly straightened up into a serious countenance and then contorted into her best damsel impression while clasping her hands together and crying, "Lock him up and throw away the key!" She pointed her finger past the officer toward Arnie in the police car. The officer turned and chuckled at the sight of Arnie with his face up to the glass. His deep, angry breaths were fogging and defogging with every dramatic inhale and exhale. "That man is a menace!" Mia added.

With her arm still extended and pointing, the officer turned back to the pair. Mia rotated her fist up and extended her middle finger at Arnie behind the officer's back. When the officer began speaking again, she snatched her arm back. "That's up to the judge, ma'am." With that, the officer returned to his vehicle and pulled away, leaving the pair alone on the street in the middle of twilight. The whole time Stephen had been staring at Mia, partially because he found her face difficult to take his eyes off of, but mostly because he was curious and entertained by her performance. The whole day had been a blur, too surreal for him to process, but this woman seemed to possess a boundless energy Stephen found alluring. Mia ignored him for a full minute, gazing at the purple and orange borealis of LA smog that coalesced in the sky above them.

"What?" Mia asked, finally meeting his eyes.

"What? I wasn't staring."

"Yes, you were, Stevo."

"I-I was somewhere else," he said, stammering.

"Oh, I bet you were."

"No, wait," he blurted out. "Stop! You keep just saying things and confusing me."

Mia chuckled, enjoying playing with him and feeding off the reaction she was getting. "Are you still interested?" Stephen's mind raced, and all his insecurities smashed into the funnel at once as he searched the events of the last three hours to find what he may have said and done that could have invited such a question. He was off. The routine was shot. Nothing had been done. The problems were stacking.

"Hey!" she called from the top of the driveway near the blue-tiled fountain. "I meant the place. Come on. I'll show you."

Mia leaned against the doorframe, watching Stephen pace the apartment. It was empty and newly painted, and the floor smelled of a fresh finish. He stepped out of his shoes and rubbed the wood with his foot through his bright white socks, then smiled in approval. "The floors are new, by the way," Mia added. Stephen put his hands in his pockets and felt right at home. "It's nice."

She yawned, the excitement of the day catching up with her. "We used to have carpets in here, but Arnie's particular taste in pets did a lot of damage."

"How can you be so cool about what happened earlier?" Stephen remarked as he began to pace again.

Mia crossed her arms and took a few steps into the room, looking at the floor, and then up at her prospective tenant, "Not the first time it's happened. Arnie's like a movie you've seen a million times. Nothing surprises you anymore. He's a loon, but harmless, and, best of all, predictable." She stopped with a foot of air between them, which made Stephen uncomfortable since he couldn't remember the last time he had been on a date, much less alone with a woman. "The exterminator would disagree." Mia rolled her eyes and said, "Billy's fine. He just got in the way of his tantrum. That's not the first time he's been hit by something Arnie's chucked at him."

Stephen backed up a few steps, only to have Mia close the gap. He crossed his arms and asked, "What kind of 'pets' did crazy but 'harmless' Arnie have?" Mia smiled big, making her lip rings look like fangs extending from those pearly white teeth. "Are you sure you want to know?" She raised her hands and wiggled her fingers while sticking out her tongue. Then, in a deep voice, she said, "You know, the kind people like to squish under their boots. The creepy *crawly* kind."

"*Crawly*," the word squirmed past all his other thoughts, worries, and problems, down through the funnel and into the sump of his fear centers. Involuntarily, his heart rate quickened, blood flushed his face, and his muscles tightened. Stephen blinked five times in succession, feeling his mouth go dry and his throat constrict, making his words crack like a teenager when he finally asked, "A... Are all these 'pets' gone?"

Stephen started to back up into the room and towards the floor-to-ceiling window at the rear wall. Mia matched him, ignoring his need for space. "Some of them. There's stragglers." That revelation ejected a film of sweat from every pore in his back and suddenly made Stephen feel cold. "Billy was going to finish them off, but Arnie interrupted." Her eyes scanned him up and down. "You all right, Stevo? You look pallid." Eager to change the subject, Stephen hugged his chest tighter and cupped his elbows with each hand firmly. "Were you guys a thing?" *Where did that come from?* He thought, *I'm not interested in this woman; why do I care? There are "crawly" things here!* His mind oscillated between repulsion and attraction.

"A *thing?*" Mia followed up, snatching Stephen away from his inner monologue.

Having almost forgotten there was another person in the room, Stephen stammered, shook his head, closed his eyes, and finally remembered what the conversation was about. "Uh, you know, like a couple. Usually guys don't act like that for just anybody." Mia darted her eyes to the side and frowned while nodding slowly. "I think at this juncture that would be none of your business, Stevo." Stephen had been somewhere else for so long he hadn't noticed he was still retreating and Mia was still pursuing him. His back bumped against the window at the rear wall, and Mia continued until she was looking up at him with not much between them. Out of space, Stephen stretched his neck back to give his head some room to look down at Mia, crunching his chin into his chest to do so. "Never mind. Look, I don't know about this place. It looks great but—"

"You're afraid of Arnie?" She interrupted.

"No," he snapped back with a tinge of annoyance. Mia's eyes narrowed up at him, and she smiled. "What's the problem?" she whispered, leaning closer with her lips an inch from his compressed chin. "Afraid of *bugs?*"

At the mention of *that*, Stephen's heart rate peaked, and adrenaline shot through his blood stream, making his body straighten up with his fists balled up at his side. He stepped forward, finally backing Mia off and making her take two steps back. Her eyes went wide with surprise, but not fear. "I don't *like bugs! I hate them,*" he yelled. Collecting himself immediately, Stephen lowered his voice and stretched his neck to the side to relieve tension, and after a pause, he said, "I don't need the drama. I just came up here because I didn't just want to walk off like a dick after what happened."

"Stevo."

"What?" He replied, throwing off his train of thought.

"Don't be a pussy. Once Billy gets all fixed up, I'll get him back over here, and he'll go all Chernobyl on the whole complex." Mia held up her hand and wiggled her little finger. "Pinkie swear. As for Arnie, he's in jail, getting butt-surfed by whichever ethnicity is desperate enough to do the deed. Happy?"

Stephen wanted to laugh but was still uneasy about what could still be lurking within the crevices of the place. The stranger in him, however, felt a yearning to stay. Mia's smile and humor invited something out of his head that Stephen wanted to explore and get to know. He grinned. "Are you always this honest?"

"It's the law, isn't it? And I'm the manager. I could have lied about the bugs, but I didn't." She clasped her hands behind her back, bent over, and batted her eyelashes. "Doesn't that buy me brownie points, Stevo?" Stephen looked down, abruptly shy and a little embarrassed about losing his temper but wanting to laugh at Mia's uninhibited display. "You have to tell me everything. It's called full disclosure."

Mia straightened and arranged her hands around an imaginary

shotgun blasting recoil her way. "Like if some guy went ape shit and gave his old battle axe both barrels and the walls a new coat of paint?"

With that, she broke him, and out of the crack came a nervous laugh: "Jesus. You're terrible at this!"

Mia cocked her arm back and slammed her finger at him. "See! I finally got you to unclench your butt cheeks and live a little. So, you want the place or what? There's a lot of starving actors interested." Stephen was self-conscious again, wondering if he had let something slip. And if so, what else was he saying about himself that he didn't want anyone to know? "Who said I was an actor?"

"Isn't everyone a failed actor here?"

"Well, you have to try to fail. I haven't even started."

She clapped her hands, the loud slap echoing around the room and startling Stephen. "I was right! See, we can smell our own! What's it going to be, Stevo? In or out?"

Stephen puffed out a breath and decided to solve problem one. "I'm in. But you have to get your boy in here to gas the place. I'm not responsible for what I'll do if I wake up in a sea of those," the thought made him lift his nostrils as though he had caught whiff of a rotting corpse, causing his gorge to rise at the back of his throat, "*things*."

Mia crossed her arms and met them with an exaggerated bow of her head. "I will make it so."

"Mother fucker is lucky I got probation; otherwise, I'd choke out that blue-haired twink," Billy mumbled out loud around the cigarette crunched between his teeth while grunting under the weight of his tools and bug sprayers. "I have no idea what Mia saw in that dude."

It had been a week since that short prick caught him slipping and bounced one of Mia's glass prayer candles off his head. *Why the fuck did that bitch have Jesus candles anyway? She ain't religious. Whatever,* he thought. The wound had cut deep, required stitches, and came with a steep bill he didn't have insurance to pay. Another reason he planned to tax ol' Arnold- if he had the sand to come around again. *I'll get paid back. You watch that shit.*

Billy set down his tanks behind his beat-up 1968 Ford pickup that sported a Chinook camper shell that, at this point, looked like it had grown out of and melted back into the vehicle's chassis rather than having been placed on it. The vehicle tripled as his work van, mobile office, and apartment. Speaking of that, where was he going to park to relax for the night? Hollywood cops were always on the prowl for dudes squatting in their trucks, and he couldn't afford another ticket, much less getting run for the warrants on the ones he already had.

"Fuck it," he coughed. Billy wiggled out of his overalls and kicked them to the side, then yanked open the door to the rear of his camper shell. A cloud of nicotine, lingering over his widow's peak, caught the loosening rust from the frame. He waved it all away and squinted into the interior of his camper. The setting sun had dipped down to touch the Pacific Ocean, throwing a long, opaque shadow behind his camper that made it nearly impossible to focus. Billy gripped both sides of the door frame and had one foot on the bumper, about to hoist himself in, when he heard movement at the back of the truck. It wasn't any of his gear shifting or the vehicle settling; he had been living in this thing for years; he knew all its aches and pains like his own. No, someone or something was in there.

Backing away a few steps, Billy puffed out his chest, feeling a little foolish that he was standing in the street in soiled boxers, a brown-should-be-white tank top, and his cigarette hanging off the corner of his mouth, spackled in saliva. "If anyone is in there, they're getting fucked up," he yelled with bass in his voice as he balled up his fists.

A familiar voice squeaked along the plastic and metal of the camper, then out to assault Billy's eardrums, instantly quickening his courage at the thought of planting his boot in the mouth of the one who issued it. "You think I am going to let you get away with killing my *babies*?"

Billy blinked and cocked his head to one side in disbelief. *Arnie?! Is that fuckin' Arnie?* "Cocksucker, get out of my truck!" Having lost all fear of the unknown and anticipating a quick dopamine fix, Billy stomped his socks back to the rear of the camper and was about to lurch himself into it at the little rodent when the afternoon orange slid across something shiny and chrome coming out of the dark at him. It swiped under his vision and almost made him laugh at the thought of Arnie's little hands trying to keep Billy away, but then he felt a warm wetness down the front of his tank top and looked down.

Streams of crimson were spewing down his chest and pooling on the concrete. He felt his chest and brought up a hand painted red. It was then that he realized that Arnie had killed him. Billy smiled to himself and scoffed through a partially shorn larynx at the thought that, *Of all the shit that could do me in, it's fuckin' Arnie. Fuck my life.*

With that, his eyes rolled back and his legs gave out, causing him to pitch face first into the bed of the camper. The last sensations his brain registered before shutting down were a violent jerk, the dragging of his body, and the sound of the door shutting him into darkness.

Stephen was calm and impressed with himself. After solving Problem One within two days of arriving in LA, he moved on to the next challenge, securing employment. He didn't want to entertain Problem Three since that possibility was so remote as to be impossible. For now, Stephen was content that he had progressed so far from his sessions and his arresting anxieties. Plus, the auditory hallucinations had lessened with his new dose.

His eyes traveled over his new place and the few sealed boxes he had containing his possessions, a couple of which were doubling for his chair and table so he could enjoy his feast out of white Chinese food cartons. He had come so far out of his comfort zone that he had the courage to travel to a whole other state to pursue a career his mother would have said "a *little crawler* like him would have no chance of being successful in." Mother had often said when she had forced him to sing in the church choir that neither he nor the other "*little cockroaches*" could hold a tune and that they were offending the Lord by barely counting as humans.

Stephen looked down into his carton of greasy noodles and thought, *Why did I get Chinese? I hate Chinese! She loved Chinese. I always thought noodles looked like worms. I told her that, and she made me eat them anyway.* The association made his stomach turn, relieving him of his appetite and making him push the carton as far from himself as possible.

Avoiding the tendency to ruminate over his mother, Stephen looked at the Hollywood skyline through his floor-to-ceiling window. One thing he could not get used to about being in such a hive of activity was the constant hum of traffic and the sound of helicopters buzzing around his place. The city was always alive, undulating, and moving. The traffic at night resembled ribbons of fireflies intertwining and flowing underneath each other in the ever-persistent drive for resources and the objects of their instincts. Stephen thought about what that would sound like. *Would it be graceful, like the music of air rushing under their wings? Or something more gross, like their little bodies rubbing together mid-flight. Like a gooey, greasy sound lubricated by ejaculates from who knows where on those inhuman bodies.*

The hum was suddenly not so distant and confined to the concrete patrol paths but individuated right near him. He heard it—a slithering mass. They were wet and writhing over each other in a disgusting ball of biomass that had no beginning nor end. The sound stabbed him in the back of his throat and skewered his gag reflex, making him almost eject the worms he had eaten earlier.

Stephen pressed his hand tightly to his mouth and ran for the bathroom, where he dumped the shaving kit into the sink. He sifted through toiletries until he came up with his amber bottle with the white cap. He struggled with the child-proof seal and managed to get the recommended dose down his throat before the desire to vomit almost overtook him.

Mia opened her door enough to stick her face through to look Stephen up and down before flashing those pearls at him while cocking an eyebrow. "Stevo, what can I do for you?"

"Are you hearing any strange noises? Like in the walls?" He was clean, showered, and shaved, but still looked disheveled and agitated.

"Like what sort of noises in the walls, Stephen?" She replied, knowing the answer.

It took Stephen a minute to follow up. He scratched his head, tugged at his collar, and looked shiny. After collecting himself, he cracked, "Like, something is moving around." He lifted his hands between them and imitated Mia's wiggly fingers. She looked at his hands jiggling in front of her face. Then back to Stephen. She went blank, narrowed her eyes, and frowned. "Ah, ha, I see what you're doing, Stevo. I see what you're up to." She opened the door and stepped out of her apartment towards him, wagging her winger in his face.

Stephen stayed planted in his netherworld of phobias and didn't register that she was in his space again until she was right on him. "What are you talking about?" He snapped.

She dropped her hand and leaned in with wide eyes. "Is that the best excuse you could come up with to knock on my door?"

"What? No, you said that Arnie had bugs, so..."

"I did?" She cut in.

Eager to convince her and calm himself, Stephen followed up, "You were very explicit! You said, 'creepy crawly.'" He wiggled his fingers again for emphasis. Mia huffed out a breath and snorted, "That sounds kind of gay. I'm not sure I would say something like that."

That's it, Stephen thought. He had had enough of feeling vulnerable and embarrassed. "Whatever," he said in a slightly elevated and confident tone, "never mind!" He performed an about face and stomped away, then stopped in his tracks when he heard Mia let out a laugh. Stephen turned and saw her bent over, gripping her knees and amused by the show she was putting on, catching him awkwardly among undulating emotions of embarrassment, anger, and frustration. She straightened and coughed, "I'm joking, dude. Come on in." Mia spun on her heels, kicked open her door, then disappeared into her apartment.

Stephen shut the door behind him and called out into the unfamiliar space, "Hello?" Mia's head popped out from the kitchen. "I saw Billy's van before I left on my errands." After that, her face was out of sight again, tending to clinking glass and heavy thuds on the linoleum counter. "I'm sure whatever's left is the last of its kind. Better?"

"Well, maybe it's just me then." He said. He was examining a piece of black fabric, nailed above some crates of vinyl records next to a turntable and adorned with a white Celtic knot.

"What?" She yelled, amidst her clinking in the kitchen. Stephen had bent over to lift the needle arm from the turntable with his finger. "Nothing." Mia walked out of the kitchen carrying two glasses full of red wine. "Don't touch that." He snatched back his hand and joined the other in his pockets. "I'm having wine, and so are you," she said after jamming the glass to his chest.

"No, I shouldn't." Mia lifted the glass up beneath his nose, wafting the pungent odor of Northern California grapes up his nostrils. "I would drink alone, but since you're here, I can at least lie to myself and say that I am not an alcoholic." He took the glass and raised it. Mia matched him and drained hers in one gulp.

"So, what did you do?"

"After I informed said producer that I would not be making a home for his seminal fluids, I kindly told him to blow himself. He was not pleased."

"That's why you're not acting anymore?"

"Nah, I was tired of it by then. I was going to quit regardless. It just so happened at the same time I landed the gig as the manager of this comfy spot, which includes free rent, so here I am, and here I've been."

They were sitting on the floor between the couch and the coffee table. Next to two empty glasses sat a drained bottle of wine. Stephen felt warm and drowsy. He wondered if there was some interaction going on within his body that he would pay for later. *Later can wait*, he thought.

"So, what misfortune brought you to LA?" Mia asked.

The alcohol was making him feel floaty and euphoric enough to forget himself a bit, but her question brought him right back to his anxieties and raised his defenses: "Who says anything happened? Maybe I just got up and decided to move." Stephen had been looking at the wall directly in front of him and focusing on that Celtic knot for so long that he hadn't noticed Mia had scooted so close. When he turned his head toward her, she was nearly in his face.

"Oh, come on, Stevo. People move here to escape. Everyone has problems." She widened her eyes and said, "Look at me." He looked away and remembered the teenager who assured him he would "fit in" here in LA. "I had a kind of breakdown. I started hearing things." Stephen's eyes were on the wall, and his mind was assessing all the possible responses. There was a long silence that drew his eyes back to Mia, who was staring at him blankly. "So, you're crazy?"

Her terse reply broke the tension and made Stephen breathe out a small laugh, then look away again. "Clinically, yes. Everything up to my thirty-first birthday was fine, then, snap, I started hearing weird stuff."

"Like voices telling you to burn shit? Or kill hookers?" Stephen was so lost in his thoughts that her caustic words didn't register.

"I don't hear voices. I hear things that drive me, well," he said, looking at her, "insane." Mia was scrutinizing him again. "I'm not dangerous or anything. I take medication to level me out." She greeted that with a grin and said, "Naturally."

Had he said too much? The assumption that she was forming some opinion about him that he couldn't access was speeding up his brain, slamming past conclusions, and giving him palpitations.

He tensed up and looked down, trying to appear like he had it together when he really didn't. *Don't lose it. You don't need this. Things are going well.* He was balling up his fists, and his anger was rising, squeezing out beads of sweat down his spine. *That fucking bitch! It's all her fault. If she were here, I'd take that bucket and shove it up her ass! I'd stomp her into the dirt!*

I'd make sure she could never get up and hurt me every again! She's the reason I'm a schizoid loser. Look at me; I can't even sit here with a pretty woman without...

Stephen felt something pointed and hard running down the side of his head. A foreign body, not perspiration, that at first he thought was a bug. Perhaps a tiny mite tapping its spiky little limbs over his pores and the contours of his skin, looking for someplace to burrow? The thought almost made him spring to his feet and run screaming from the place, slapping himself all over.

The turn of his head made him see it was Mia sliding the tip of her nail on his skin and then extending her fingers to cup the whole of his jaw. Her touch soothed him and lowered his heart rate. He studied her face. She wasn't looking at his eyes but at his entire aspect. "You know, Stephen," now that her hand had slipped around his neck and gripped the back of his head, "I have a thing for strange fellows like you."

"Schizoid losers?" Mia started to crawl on top of him, making him lean back on one arm away from her oncoming lips. "Beats losers with exotic tastes in weird pets."

His hand slipped on the hardwood floor and made him fall on his back. Mia was over him now, hands planted on either side of his head, her hair hanging low and tickling his cheeks. "Weird?"

"The one I got hostage. Bitch cost two grand. That's what Arnie owes me. And that's what I'm getting back." Mia was down now, nibbling on his chin and clocking him with predatory eyes. "So, that's what all that was about."

"You're a fast one, Stephen."

"Would you not call me Stephen? My mother called me that."

"Shut up." She said, as she sealed his mouth with hers.

Before Stephen's thoughts could drain out of his mind towards his other regions, he enjoyed the fleeting triumph that Problem Three had been solved.

This worthless meat bag smells as bad as he did when he was alive, Arnie thought as he wiped his own naked body down with greasy towels. He had been living in Billy's camper for a week, and the Southern California summer wasn't making it pleasant. Billy's body had ripened and started to become host to decomposers whose emissions were breaking through the plastic Arnie had wrapped him in. Not even the broken cigarettes he had shoved up his nose were enough to block the smell.

Still, he had a rescue mission to pull off, and he wasn't going to let something like his cunt ex-girlfriend or a body he didn't risk getting rid of on account of putridity stop him.

Every so often, Arnie had to crack open the camper's rear door to exchange some air—and occasionally vomit— when something unpleasant wafted up from Billy's postmortem flatulence. This time it was a combination of the miasma and the sounds of Mia and Stephen's sloppy lovemaking emanating from his surveillance setup.

Arnie wasn't savvy enough for video, but he had managed to plant a microphone in Mia's place a few months before she went on her insecticide. She had gotten all of his rare pets, *that bitch*, but she took the crown jewel hostage. An insect so rare that not many know about it. *My queen*, he thought, *I scraped and stole to make you mine, and I won't let some tall asshole or that gash take you from me. I'll get even with both of you before I abscond with her.*

When he tried his old key and it turned the lock, Arnie felt vindication tickle his pride and conjure memories of how Mia used to ridicule and condescend him. Here he was with his tools, and that moron hadn't even changed the locks! *That's the last time you underestimate me, slut,* he thought, remembering all those incidents of her standing over him and making fun of his height and stature, causing him to feel small and akin to the objects of his passion.

She claimed that that very passion made him interesting, only to turn around and destroy the very thing that gave his life meaning. All those feelings of invalidation and inferiority, coupled with his own sense of stunted superiority, coalesced into a potent brew that fueled the anticipation of revenge against the *new guy*. As he pushed open the door to Stephen's apartment, Arnie giggled.

It was just how Stephen had left it. Boxes and left-over Chinese. Arnie had a little pen light he had found amongst Billy's beat-up tools. He smacked it against his palm to stop it from flickering and moved the beam over to the kitchen counter, where he spotted a lone manilla envelope. Arnie opened it and spilled out a stack of eight and a half by eleven glossies of that schmuck who had moved into his place, then between Mia's legs.

"Typical, this fucking guy would be an actor. How cliche," he scoffed to himself in a low voice. *Look at this guy,* he fumed. *Chad looks like every other asshole in this city. Tall, lean, and full of hair. You might as well throw on some pooka shells! He's so..."* Normal!" Arnie nearly ripped the stack in two, uttering that word he found so repugnant, but steeled himself as the means, and the end he desired so deeply mattered more than desecrating a photo of a future Mr. GQ.

He returned the head shots to the envelope and lurked along into the bathroom, where Stephen's shaving kit had been left on the floor with its contents still dumped into the sink. "What a slob," he whispered, moving the pen light over the sink to the amber bottle with the white cap Stephen had left behind. He picked it up and turned it within the piss-yellow glow of the pen light. "Not so normal after all. Let's see if we can bump it up a notch."

Arnie popped the top and emptied the remaining pills into the toilet, flushing it afterwards. Then he reached into his stinky jumpsuit and removed a sandwich bag full of a rainbow of shapes, sizes, and colors. "Billy, you continue to serve me even in compost," he laughed, fishing out some matching pills. Arnie funneled the ringers into the bottle and left it just as he found it.

"That should keep Chad busy while I get back what's mine!"

Two weeks. Only two weeks, and I've got a place and a girlfriend. I think. After brushing his hair and putting on a new sport coat, Stephen paused to reflect in the mirror on his progress, realizing that he had come a long way from his lifelong slumber. Now that he had tackled Problems One and Three, it was time to relentlessly tackle the second one, driven by his success.

Everything was in order. He had avoided the urge to stay on the floor with Mia all day and had slipped out to shower, clean up, and call a cab, so he was at his first audition bright and early. Stephen guessed that up above the haze that settled on the city during weekday traffic, the stars were aligning on his behalf, and he wasn't about to insult whatever physics were at work with complacency.

With keys and headshots in hand, Stephen was heading for the door when he realized he had forgotten the most important thing. The thing that could derail everything, draw the entire world past his new-found confidence, and reveal that just under the surface, he was still a roiling carpet of insecurities and traumas while being prone to auditory derangement.

With the door open, he ran back to the bathroom, grabbed his pills, popped the cap, and dry swallowed. The sensation gave him pause. That one seemed larger than his normal dose, and his throat had a hard time with it, expecting something smaller. He shrugged and attributed the strangeness to the fact that he was nervous and his throat was dry from a night of imbibing alcohol. *Better get some water in me so I don't get dry mouth*, he anticipated as he walked out the door.

Stephen was a little confused and agitated. He'd had a great night last night and an even better morning. Everything went well getting out from under Mia and then out of the house, plus there was zero traffic on the way to the casting office, a rarity for LA. It was in the elevator leading up to his first audition that he started to feel a pulsating heat behind his eyeballs, followed by disorientation. His heart got going, and he was anxious. It wasn't the typical bout of nerves anyone would have going in for a job interview, but something he couldn't understand that was sitting in the pit of his stomach and stoking a slow-burn terror within him.

Maybe the excitement of the last forty-eight hours was catching up with him. Stephen wasn't used to whirlwind romances, so maybe that and the interactions from the alcohol were playing hell with his body chemistry. All these suspects were circling the funnel of his mind as he sat in the lobby with the other hopefuls biting on his thumbnail and bouncing his knee to a phantom rhythm.

Why now? I was fine all morning. He thought through the tightening of his chest and back, like he was stuck in a slowly dilating bottle that was rapidly filling and drowning him in his own anxiety. *Something's stacking, and by all rights, it shouldn't be. And it's freaking me out!*

Then he heard it. A loud clicking sound, like two hollow wooden planks being smacked together. It was so sudden, like the crack of lightning across the darkening skies of his inner world, that it made him jump in his seat and cock his head from side to side to locate it. Click.

This time, it felt like razor blades sliding rupturing channels across his eardrums. Stephen knew when he was having auditory hallucinations, but this was something he had not experienced before. The hallucinations felt amplified and all-encompassing, rather than distant and localized, even though they could truly be occurring. This felt like his brain was swelling two to three times its size, pressing against his skull, popping out his eye balls.

Click, click, in close succession.

It sounded like the *tap, tap, tapping* of the extremities of something sharp.

Armored.

Biological.

Mandibles, he thought. Sounds like when these disgusting little creatures are rubbing themselves with those inhuman limbs and they chitter with ecstasy, like one would scratch an itch.

"Fuck!" Stephen huffed out.

"Did you say something?" Came the reply.

He looked at the fashionista cum secretary at her desk, scrutinizing him over the top of her magazine. She was clicking her long red nails together with her other hand. Knowing the source, Stephen's mind dialed down the volume and his terror a tad, allowing him enough composure to nod and put her right back to ignoring him.

Stephen was shivering with sweat, and he could feel his eyelids stapled to his forehead. He rubbed the sides of his temples and calmed down when the clicking started up again. He glanced at the secretary, only to find her free hand now occupied with a latte. His eyes crawled away from her, along the desk, to the floor, and across the seating area to the other pseudo-actors. Guys, mothers, girls...

Wait, his mind grabbed the steering sticks of his ocular capacity and yanked them back over a young blond woman, mouthing her lines to herself. Between her and a muscular, tanned surfer guy sat a tacky old hag wearing a yellow moomoo dress and sporting a tall, blue beehive hairdo. Wreathed in cigarette smoke and ancient, the bespectacled crone looked as out of place as a wheelchair-bound dwarf would be sitting between Mr. Olympia and Miss America. Her cigarette bloomed behind a limp and way too long cherry of ash, followed by a phlegm-laden cough amidst a mushroom cloud plume coalescing with spit particles.

Stephen couldn't believe it, nor could he look away or blink. The sight of Mother blasted him back into his seat. *But that's impossible; she's dead! The bitch is dead and buried back in that shithole I came from.* His eyes managed to tick a little down to the plastic bucket she had cradled in her other arm. Through the foggy container roiled a dark coagulation of limbs, eyes, and antennae in a cacophonous dance that punched Stephen in the gut and made him cough and nearly empty his stomach. Mother tapped the end of her cigarette and let the ash fall to the floor with the sound of a sledge hammer, whose mnemonic resonance sounded memories of all the times his face, arms, and back were under those smoldering embers. Finally, his mother looked at him through her cheap gold-rimmed glasses and spoke in a deep, masculine voice, "You got a problem, buddy?"

"Stephen?" With a clip board and pen in hand, the casting assistant loomed, pulling him out of his psychosis and back into the room where a photocopy of every handsome male hopeful in LA had replaced Mother. Taking stock of himself, Stephen felt humid under his clothes and his mouth so dry that he could barely get out the words, "Yeah?"

"We're ready for you." He nodded and followed on after her, leaving the photocopy to mutter an observation to his counterpart next to him: "What a fag."

What is that? Stephen wondered after following the casting assistant down a narrow hall to her boss' office. *It was so loud*, like the sound of an excavator dumping a ton of pebbles onto the concrete floor of a nitroglycerin plant. It was so deafening that he was surprised she couldn't hear it. Part of him knew this was in his head, but that section of himself that still had a hold of reality was quickly receding to nothing in the rear view of his rapidly unfolding trip to lunacy.

In front of him, the hallway stretched to a tiny pinhole of light, and the walls on either side of him bulged with convex indentations on their surface that pulsated like they were walking down the throat of some massive creature. The sound grew louder, and painfully so. Upon closer inspection, he noticed billions of cockroaches, each creating tiny dimples beneath the now-paper-thin surface, threatening to burst and roll over him in a suffocating wave of crunch and squealing.

"Are you all right?" Her question slammed his visions back with a thump, like the abrupt return of a measuring tape.

"May I use the bathroom, please?"

Stephen threw up what remained in his stomach and proceeded to work in the cupboard under the sink. He was with it again, but paranoid. He rummaged and came up with a can of bug spray. He stared at the arrogant little cartoon ant on the label. *It* was standing at attention with a salute. *It* was attired in a stahlhelm with a lightning bolt along its side. *It* thought it was the master race and could victimize anyone! Stephen's eyes narrowed, and he declared through clenched teeth, "Alright, fuckers. You've been after me my whole life. Come and get it!" With that, he wrapped his headshots around the can and opened the door.

"Sit, sit, sit. Let's get this going."

As ordered, Stephen sat himself down in a folding chair in front of the wooden desk of the casting director, who didn't bother to look up from his script to regard the candidate. "No need to go crazy here," he repeated for the tenth time that day, "this is just for Drug Dealer Number Four. You have five lines. Go!" *A real Stanislavski we got here. Waiting on this guy to drench himself in the bathroom better have been worth it*, he mused while grinning at the pretension of the "actor" in front of him, who was clearly going all in for this gig.

Stephen couldn't blink, and his eyes burned from dryness, even when moisturized by the beads of sweat that were rolling down from his hairline. He'd studied his five lines over and over again, repeating them on the toilet, in the shower, and to himself on the cab ride over, but couldn't get them out. His brain was rapidly creating and perceiving, making even mundane tasks like reading symbols on paper nearly impossible.

He opened his mouth to speak, but he stuttered while gripping the headshot roll so tightly that the sound of his palm sliding around it was loud enough to raise the curiosity of the casting director. Without moving his head, he looked up, dropped the script with a slap on the desk, shrugged, and asked, "Are we doing this?" *Why are all these losers wasting their precious time? Just out with it already! It's a bit part. A day player for Christ-sakes!*

Stephen dried his face with his sleeve and was able to blink, then went to speak but was interrupted by that damn clicking. It was behind him this time, drawing him to twist in his chair and see Mother sitting on the couch with that bucket. "So, you want to be an actor, huh?" She coughed.

I hate fuckin' actors, the casting director thought. *If physical bullshit is what he needs to get through his lines, then fine*, "What's that over there?"

The casting director read off his script in a flat voice. Stephen was still looking away while watching Mother finish her cigarette and put it out in the bucket. The mound of cockroaches chirped and scattered, some of them scurrying over the lip and onto the couch.

"Holy shit," Stephen whispered.

The casting director was thrown off by this guy going off script: "Wrong line, but we're liberal here with the improv." *Jesus,* "'I think we got cops. Better tell the boss.'"

Mother was on her feet, carrying the bucket towards Stephen. "You think you can scurry away from me?"

"I-I didn't." The casting director rolled his eyes up to see Stephen looking to his side. *On some kind of upper too, I see.* He snapped his fingers and said, "Hey, that's not the line." Mother was halfway to where Stephen was sitting, still breathing out smoke despite not smoking a cigarette. The smell of nicotine mixed with body odor almost made him retch right there, but the terror of a thousand horrors doubling over each other in that bucket froze his bowels and stilled his stomach. The chair held his entire being in suspense, waiting for what lay ahead. What had come next a hundred times. "You're no better than your father!" She spat, ejecting warm droplets onto his forehead and slightly misting his arid eyeballs.

"I'm not crazy," he screamed.

I think you might be. I remember when we used to vet these assholes through agents. Annoying-ass directors think they're going to find the next red carpet moron by making these things "open." Cheap pricks, just pay someone bankable to complete the damn package!

She was over him, and Stephen was six years old again, looking up at those eyes bereft of maternal warmth, that mouth breathing hellfire, and that blue hive stuck to her head that went on forever. "You've been a very bad boy, Stephen." His voice rang out in a prepubescent tone: "You're dead, mother! Leave me alone!"

What the fuck was that? The casting director thought as he pushed his chair back. *Enough*, "All right, buddy, I think we got it. We'll be in touch." Stephen shot up from his chair and ripped something from the same hand that was holding the headshot roll. He threw those aside without looking. They floated everywhere and rained down on the casting director like confetti. "Yo, did you hear me? We're done! And pick all that shit up on the way out." Stephen wasn't listening; he wasn't there; he was standing up to the monster in front of him. He was doing what he should have done rather than letting nature save him. Stephen raised the can of bug spray in front of him.

That's it! I've had enough of this project! It's lunchtime! My blood sugar's low! These patches aren't working. My wife's banging on my assistant! This psycho's got to go! The casting director stomped around his desk to this dolt holding up bug spray like a cross, warding off an imaginary vampire, and slapped his palm on his shoulder, scrunching up Stephen's blazer and yanking him around. "Boy, I told you to..."

Stephen whipped around into the mouth of the clear bucket, coughing forth a brown and black horde of flesh and disease. They swarmed him, wrapping around his head in one mass and using their combined strength of a million arms to pry over his nasal cavity, tear duct, mouth, and ear lobes. *My God*, he thought in total terror, *they're boring me out from inside; there's going to be nothing left of me!*

Stephen shrieked, slapped his own face five or six times like one of the Three Stooges, then whipped up the bug spray and gave the casting director a full blast from the pressurized can. He flew back, stumbling on his feet and rubbing his chemically burned eyes. The top of his legs smacked into the desk and doubled over it, sending him face first onto the floor.

Behind Stephen, the door flew open, and a humanoid cockroach stomped into the room. Its bulk could barely get through the frame, and its antennae scraped the panels of the drop ceiling. It surveyed the room by rotating its head from left to right while emitting that enraging clicking sound. "What the hell is going on in here?" it chirped. Stephen was going to blast it, but his can of bug spray was dry. *Maybe I can distract it and just dart past!*

He tossed the can as hard as he could at what he thought was the mutant cockroach's face, then sprinted just ahead of it. *It worked!* He thought, as he looked over his shoulder to catch that the monster roach had vanished and left behind one of the male interns out cold on the floor with the expended can rolling around his head.

Stephen ran past the other actors, the fashionista's desk, and a delivery man who just happened to have the door open to aid in his escape. "Fuuuuuuuuuuucccck!" he yelled as he gained speed.

As Stephen's profanity waned down the hall, the Photocopy Chad looked to his doppelgänger next to him, repeating the same five lines, and noted, "Fucking method actor."

Lactic acids ate up his muscles, and his heart rate was screaming in his ears to the rapid rhythm of his heels pounding on the pavement. He could feel his capillary beds straining under the load of his life engine opening its sluice gates to spill forth adrenaline into his blood stream and fuel another mile of running at a full sprint.

The handlebars of a speeding motorcycle had caught Stephen's blazer, tearing it off his body, taking a piece of his shirt with it. His chin was glued to his neck, causing his face to contort into a frozen scream. Behind his hyper extended jaw his throat sucked down oxygen like a hot rod, drying his mouth and opening sores desperate for moisture.

The funnel had caught all the sense data and clogged it, but his rational mind managed to avoid drowning for a moment to break the surface and scream, "*STOP!*"

Stephen obeyed and dove behind the first corner he came across. He went down on one knee and closed his mouth, collapsing the wax mold of saliva that had caked around his mouth down his throat, which almost made him choke amidst the bellows that raised his back to double its size, like some cornered predator straightening its fur at the sight of a threat.

Through the drumming of blood rushing through his brain, Stephen managed to ask himself, *Where am I? I'm behind a dumpster. Did I lose her?*

"You will never lose me!" Screeched a voice through a half-human voice box behind him. The sun blinded Stephen as soon as he looked up. A giant cockroach, standing on two legs, momentarily relieved his blown out eyeballs by swarming him with its brethren.

His face contorted into a screaming rictus again, but his tired and spent throat could not issue the full force of the terror that wrapped both hands around his cerebellum and squeezed. With his primal drive still intact, Stephen channeled all his strength into a punch that struck the bulbous face of the creature, then sprinted past it as it lurched backward from the impact.

"Home, home, home! Safe, safe, safe!" He yelled down the alley at full sprint again. The cockroach rose up, clutching its very human face, and spat out a tooth. "You broke my fucking jaw, you asshole!" The vagrant yelled after his assailant around limp and wagging chops.

Mia wondered if Stephen would be back. She had gotten so loaded last night and slept so deeply that she didn't feel him slide himself away and scoot out the door. *Eh, he lives here, so he can't escape me forever,* she chuckled. She was unlocking the master lock to the communal mailbox when she saw Billy's van parked on the narrow driveway and nearly butting up against the blue and white fountain.

Unusual, Mia thought, *dude knows better than to block the driveway.* She skipped over while cupping her hands around her mouth and yelling, "Yo, Billy, did you fall asleep again?" Mia tapped a rhythm along the side of his camper shell before moving around the back and pounding a tune on Billy's silted-over back window. "Seriously, dude, I told you to sleep it off at my place. Camping on the curb will only score you another ticket, plus if the owners roll by I'll get heaps of crap."

Bet he's on one again, she assumed before yanking open the camper door. Immediately, a stench leapt out of her, which in turn brought on a cough laden with the acidic tinge of bile. Mia managed to choke it back after taking two steps. *What's Billy got in here—a dead body?* She mused, before denying all her instincts and climbing into the van, where she kneeled before what looked like a rug wrapped in plastic.

Flies buzzed around her head, and the smell was so overpowering she could barely keep her eyes open. With the tips of her fingers, she pulled a flap back to see a partially liquified Billy staring up at her. Maggots had made a nest in his eyes, and his skin was bloated around his lips, pulled tight around his yellow teeth. At the throat around grey, necrotic flesh was a gash caked in old dried blood. The shock of seeing Billy stifled a scream and sent Mia stumbling backwards towards the door, where she landed on her rear to be caught by a thin, bony arm wrapped around her waist and thin, cold steel pressed against her throat.

Arnie's familiar voice breathed out an even worse odor around her head and up her nose. "You didn't think I had it in me. Did you?" He pressed the razor blade a little and broke the skin, issuing a small bead of blood down Mia's neck. "Now you'll listen when I'm giving the orders, cunt. I don't want any shit, or I'll do to you what I did to that genocidal maniac. Give me what I want, and I'll let you live. Nod if you get me!"

She did.

Mia momentarily believed that Arnie had slashed her throat, but he had merely removed the razor; the jolt she felt was a feeble attempt to force her to the ground of her bedroom. She stumbled slightly and then wheeled to face the little pest.

Arnie waved the razor about the room and grinned, "I see you've fixed up the place." Mia wiped away the blood from the small cut on her neck. "Much easier to keep clean without your shit around."

He took a step towards her, waving the blade around for emphasis. "You didn't seem to mind it. I think the term you used to describe it was 'fascinating.'"

Mia stood her ground, lowering her head to match her former

lover's height as he approached. "Sure. Until I realized what a lunatic you are."

Arnie stopped and swiped the blade under her nose, barely missing her. He smiled when she didn't flinch. "That's very cute. I always loved that mouth on you. It's only ever been good for one thing, but we ain't got time for that," he said, backing up and spreading his arms in a dramatic pose. "Now, fetch my queen!"

Keeping her eyes on Arnie, Mia backed slowly into the room, around her bed, and toward the corner next to her sliding closet door. She blindly pushed the doors open, crouched, and slid a large mason jar from the closet floor to her feet. "This is what you want," she said, picking it up with both hands and walking towards Arnie with the jar out in front of her. "Your true love?"

Arnie's eyes lowered to the jar, and his arms dropped to his sides in quiet longing. It was dark, with webbing suspending a living blotch in the center. He almost wept while he was raising his hand with flexed fingers, beckoning as though he could feel the cold glass and the subtle vibrations of the creature nesting within. "Give her to me," he said it in a low, somber tone.

"You want it?" Mia taunted, letting go of the jar and catching it mid-drop. The fright made Arnie hop once while tearing at his hair with both hands. "Mia, Goddamnit, be careful!"

"You want it?" She asked again while jerking the jar violently in her grip. Arnie yelped and extended his arms in the hopes of catching the habitat. "Please," Arnie pleaded. "Just hand her over and I'll leave."

"Yeah?" She pulled the jar closer to her chest and safely nestled it.

"Yes." Arnie assured her. He stepped back, closed the razor and then tossed it aside. "There. Now give her to me."

"Okay, take it." Mia extended her arms and held the jar out before her. Arnie smiled and began to reach for it as Mia let go and allowed the jar to fall. It exploded on contact with the hardwood floor, sending shards of glass and dirt in all directions. Out of the wreckage of her habitat, the queen tried to crawl out from under the rubble but came under the heel of Mia's boot, which pulped her into the floor, splattering bright yellow guts in a radiating pattern around her foot.

Mia pointed at Arnie and laughed while he stood there frozen with his hands still out, still processing that she had humiliated him yet again. Once his brain registered her ridicule, he straightened up and contorted his rat-like face into a beak of compressed hate.

Since the ambush in the alley, every instinct of self-preservation, coupled with his disgust reflex, had conspired to prevent Stephen from stopping. His heart was beating so fast that he thought it would seize before he made it back to his apartment. He'd thought, *Five blocks, I can't make five blocks; I'll be dead before the end of the sidewalk.*

Once he had reached the base of the hill that twisted up to where the bungalows were hidden, he assumed there was *no way; my bones wouldn't carry me up there.* But, through his last reserves of adrenaline or sheer fear of what would crawl up on him out in the open, he was suddenly collapsing on his hands and knees in the courtyard in front of the dried-up fountain.

Stephen's body was shutting down after having shot through all its energy. He wasn't sweating anymore since he had no more salt to give, but instead had developed a dull sheen that coated him with dirt, soot, and debris from his long trek across Hollywood. The wound at his side from a biker who had sideswiped him had long coagulated over and sealed itself.

Now he was on his stomach, panting into the dirt and blowing pebbles away with each breath. "Leave me alone. Please, Mother. They bite me. They scare me. *You burn me.*" Stephen rolled over and pressed his palms to his ears. "Just keep them away." His heart was slowing, and his eyes grew heavy, allowing his limbs to slacken and his muscles to relax.

He was drifting off into a torpor when Mia's scream yanked him into a déjà vu that raised him instantly onto his feet, and drove him to dash through her front door and to the bedroom. There he saw Mother straddling Mia, cradling that *fucking bucket* in one arm and gripping the latter's throat with the other. Her hair wasn't in that blue beehive dew anymore, but it was down and messy.

Fear froze him there when his mother sprouted mandibles from the sides of her jowls and a pair of antennae shot up like stalks through the top of her head. She was laughing too, but it wasn't his mother's laugh. It was akin to that horrible squeal that Stephen had heard the first day he had visited this place. It sounded like the guy Mia had been with before.

It sounded like crazy-but-harmless Arnie, except in Mother's body. The thought of these two scheming to undermine his progress enraged him as much as the vision of her trying to crawl up from her dirt nap to snatch away the only woman who didn't look at him like a schizoid loser terrified him. As fury defrosted fear, and fired fresh vitality into his depleted body, he roared, "Leave her alone, you bitch!"

Stephen charged the cockroach and knocked it to the floor. His hatred threw a red veil over his eyes, and all he wanted was to feel the warmth of its blood on his body and a death rattle from deep within its carapace. He rolled with the thing and ended up on top. It was screaming and snapping at him, cutting him all over with its razor-sharp spines. Stephen managed to break free and land the side of his foot on its jaws, knocking it prone. It still moved, and if it moved, it could still hurt him and Mia.

He stomped and stomped until he was wet with its fluids and it no longer moved. Even then, he pressed his foot down until its brains found their way through the floorboards and soaked into the subfloor. Stephen stood over it, shedding blood from numerous cuts while panting, seeing black and wobbling on his feet. He managed to stumble and finally fall against the corner where he slid down to his ass. Mia was on her knees, crawling over Arnie's body. His skull had burst, and his brains were part of the wall paper. When she reached Stephen, she settled next to him and patted his legs. "Thanks, Stephen. I appreciate you taking care of that problem for me."

Before he fell into a coma, Stephen's mouth managed to slur out, "Told you... I don't like bugs."

THE DARK OF WHITE
BY STEVE LEE

Jonas Price crested the hilltop and took in the majestic, endless white of Bathurst Island. Even with tinted snow goggles, he had to squint to combat the sun's reflection against the ice-glazed field of snow. He turned back to regard his companions, who were trailing behind, and waved for them to pick up the pace.

"Get up here, guys!" he yelled, his voice muffled by a thick ski mask. "This view is fantastic!"

"Relax," Molly called back between huffs, "the view will still be there in thirty seconds."

Her husband, James, laughed as he climbed beside her. He enjoyed the dynamic between his lady and his good friend. Her sarcastic wit bounced off his boyish enthusiasm. While Jonas was often eager and spontaneous, Molly was more reserved. She was easily annoyed, though.

"Better be a sweet view for what we paid to get here," James said under his breath.

Molly chuckled and pushed him playfully. "I'm just glad you finally brought me on one of your adventures."

He paused for a moment to admire her. Nothing made him happier than having this wonderful woman by his side, Mrs. James Hudson. She'd been with him long before he made his fortune, and she stayed with him after. She loved him, faults and all, and he knew it.

"Me, too."

Jonas had both of his skis strapped on by the time they reached him.

"Just look," he said, sweeping his arm out to present the impressive terrain. "This is going to be the best run yet!"

"I have to admit, this is beautiful," Molly replied.

"Damn," James put it, "I bet we can go for a mile off this slope."

His wife had a finger raised before he even finished. "Don't forget we have to hoof it all the way back."

"Hmm," Jonas moaned in response, "maybe we should have taken the snowcats out. It'll be dark by the time we get back to camp."

James looked to the sky, estimating they had less than two hours of daylight left. "It'll be dark before that. We better get to the fun part."

"Way ahead of you," Jonas boasted, carving his skis into the snow.

Molly sighed. "Cool your jets, Turbo."

"Just another minute or two," James told him, "We're binding up. Enjoy that view a little while longer."

That's what Jonas did, putting a hand over his visor to gaze upon the glass-like landscape. This time he noticed something he didn't see before: movement. In the distance, he saw something traversing the white tundra. He squinched his eyes to focus. The glare made it difficult to discern, but Jonas could swear that was a person out there.

"Hey, guys," he muttered.

"Yeah, yeah, we're almost ready, for crying out loud!" Molly interrupted.

"No, not that. I think there's a person down there."

James slid next to his friend and pulled out a pair of binoculars. "Where?"

"Over there," Jonas answered, pointing to the lone figure trudging across the ice and snow.

James followed his finger and saw what his pal was referring to. "Yep, that looks like a person. Inuit, from the look of it. They know this land like the back of their hands, but I doubt even one of them would be out here in no-man's-land all alone. They might need some help."

"We should go and see," Molly said, fastening the last latch on her boot.

"Oh yeah, let's do this!" Jonas cheered, launching himself over the bluff. He accelerated quickly. Mr. and Mrs. Hudson looked at each other and shook their heads, then joined him.

As the trio glided down the lengthy hillside, a harsh wind whipped up out of nowhere. The sudden gale churned the loose powder scattered across the icy crust. Visibility was significantly reduced. The arctic blast found its way into every seam in their heavy clothing, chilling them to the bone.

"Snowplow!" Jonas yelled, followed by "Zig-zag!"

Between the ski masks, hoods, and ripping winds, his instructions were only more muffled noise. He reduced speed, and Molly raced past him with James in pursuit.

Molly's continued to speed up, gaining momentum with each passing second. She'd never gone this fast before, and she could barely see. Molly tried to put everything James had taught her into practice, but her skis were biting into the ice. She felt that if she adjusted their angle even a little, her boards could catch and snap her ankles.

James leaned forward and tucked his elbows, trying to catch up to his wife. He could see nothing but lines of white until his eyes began to discern the form of Molly materializing ahead through the speeding mist.

"Molly!" he called, but he realized the effort was futile. He couldn't even hear himself.

He leaned in even more and slid into a position parallel to hers. James put both poles into his right hand and reached for Molly with his left. She must have sensed his presence. Through the driving wind and punishing snow, Molly turned her head, locking eyes with her loving husband.

"It's going to be okay!" He yelled, still trying to get a grip on her right arm. "I got you!"

Molly's goggles fogged over as she exhaled a heavy sigh of relief.

Then she smiled at James.

For the last time.

A massive snow-covered stone came into Molly's path. Before either of them could react, it took her legs out from under her. James watched helplessly as he heard the sickening thud. His wife went spiraling into the white vortex. There was a ringing in his ears, and time slowed to a crawl as he tried to process what had happened.

Before he could come to his wits, a smaller stone fractured one of his skis, and James fell forward into a tumble. The punishing roll took him further down the hillside until he finally slid to a stop near the bottom.

He felt as if he were underwater, frozen and on fire all at once. The white was fading into darkness. Through blood and tears, James thought he saw the head of a caribou come into view, looming over him. The creature looked down at the man with fiery red eyes. Its grunting morphed into a hideous, mocking laughter.

Then the black overtook him.

The squall disappeared as fast as it came. Jonas was making his way down the slope as the precipitation thinned. He cut to a stop and took out his binoculars, examining the hillside for any signs of his friends. There was nothing. There was not a trace of Molly or James anywhere. He skied down the rest of the hill, stopping often to survey the area and yell their names.

Nothing... wait.

Scanning the area, Jonas spotted the same lone figure they'd seen before they came down the incline. It was much closer now. From this distance, he could see that it was an elderly woman. She wore a thick fur parka that enveloped everything from her head to her ankles and leaned on a girthy wooden staff bound in leather and decorated with the bones

THE DARK OF WHITE

of various small animals. Inuit, as James had predicted.

Jonas slid on his skis and used his poles to propel him toward the old woman with haste. Maybe she'd seen something that could help. He moved with all haste, never slowing until he was almost on top of her. As he crested a large drift, he could see the Inuit woman ahead, but something wasn't right. She stood motionless; arms outstretched to her sides.

"Excuse me?" Jonas called out, "Ma'am?"

No response.

He slid down the embankment and skidded to a halt a few feet away from the figure. He could now see that this was not a human being. Animal skins were lashed to a stone construct, roughly the size and shape of a person. Jonas identified it as an *inuksuk*, a type of cairn that the Inuit people constructed to serve as landmarks for travelers, as he pulled the furs away. These structures were usually built tall and large to improve visibility. This one was small, though, shorter than him.

Jonas put his binoculars to his eyes and looked all around him. There is no way that old woman could have scurried out of view in the frozen tundra, but somehow she did.

"Hello?"

He turned in circles, shouting for James, Molly, the elderly Inuit... anyone. No one responded to his pleas. He finally fell onto his rump and tossed the binoculars away, burying his head into his knees.

"Pfflt."

The snort of a large animal caught Jonas off guard. He peered up to see the nose of a hulking caribou only inches from his face. It snorted again, causing him to lose balance and fall backward. He sat up and scanned the area frantically. The beast was gone. There were no tracks in the snow. He turned back to the *inuksuk* but saw nothing. It, too, was gone. Then he heard a whisper behind him—the cracking voice of an old woman.

"Your friends are dead."

Jonas jumped and turned, a shriek escaping his lips. There was no one there. Glancing around, he could see that he was all alone in the vast white. No woman, no caribou, no inuksuk. Just himself, and the sun was beginning to disappear behind the horizon. He was frozen, alone, and afraid, and there was a terrible decision before him.

"We're all going to die out here if I don't get back to camp," Jonas muttered, justifying the rational but cruel choice he had already made. "Yeah, I'll get back to camp, radio emergency, grab some supplies, and get back out here to cover more ground."

Jonas secured his goggles, pulled his hood tight, and began the arduous march back to base camp.

James opened his aching eyes. After blinking away most of the blurriness, he found that he was staring at light and shadow dancing across the pale blue ice overhead. There was a strong metallic, salty taste in his mouth.

Blood.

He tried to sit up but abandoned that notion when he realized that his upper body was stiff and sore to a degree that he'd never felt. He had no feeling from the waist down. James moaned as he turned his head to try and catch a glimpse of where he was. It appeared to be a natural tunnel, its stone glazed over by a thin layer of frozen moisture. He could feel the warmth of a fire nearby, but the flames were outside his field of vision. Someone had to have lit it.

"Hello?" James choked out weakly.

He heard shuffling behind him. Something was stirring, but if it was a human being, they weren't responding to his plea.

"Please," he whimpered, "please answer. I... I can't feel my legs. Am I going to die?"

"Of course not, darling." The comforting voice of his wife came back.

"Molly?" James croaked in disbelief, rolling over despite the pain, in order to see his beloved. There she stood, waving her hands over a large fire to warm them. She had removed her coat, and her long, dark hair fell over her back and shoulders. Her eyes were closed, and her face looked strangely peaceful considering their current situation.

"Yes, husband. We made it."

James's expression soured as he recalled the last time he saw her. "But… I thought…"

"Thought what, dear?"

"I thought... you died, Molly. You hit that rock like a bullet."

Molly laughed at his assertion, something James found both strange and unsettling.

"No, darling. It was pure chaos in that squall. Your eyes were playing tricks on you, silly."

His head was still swimming, and the pain was affecting him on multiple levels. Still, James couldn't shake the feeling that something was off about this exchange. This woman looked like his wife and sounded like her too, but she did not speak like the woman he married. It felt like a dream. As if someone else were speaking through Molly's mouth. The stabbing aches were real, though, and he knew what he saw.

"What's going on here?" James asked sharply.

"I don't know what you mean, husband."

"Where is Jonas?" he demanded.

"Darling, I didn't see..."

"Say my name!" James shouted, taking note of the pet names she was using. Molly was more likely to call him 'dummy' than darling. Especially in trying circumstances. It was her way of easing the tension.

"What?" the woman replied, seemingly taken aback by his abrupt change of tone.

"What's my name, Molly?" he asked again, slowly.

She smiled and opened her eyes, revealing the fiery red orbs beneath the lids. The woman moved to stand over James and leered down at him.

"You are cleverer than most," she said, her voice lowering into a whispering hiss. "Even with a concussed brain. Impressive."

James's eyes went wide, and he recoiled at her approach, but whatever this creature was, he was at her mercy. His beaten body would not allow for any heroics. He took a deep breath, summoning the strength to endure whatever was about to happen.

"Where is my wife?"

"Dead," the creature told him with a taunting smirk, "but you already knew that."

James winced at the inevitable news and closed his eyes tightly to fight back the tears.

"And Jonas?"

"Your other companion has abandoned you."

He shook his head. "No. I don't believe that. He's going for help."

"He is saving his own skin," the creature told him. She took his neck and squeezed it with a strength Molly's petite frame should not possess. "Your fate is mine to decide, *dear husband*."

"What is it you want?" James inquired, "Money?"

Her sinister cackle split the frigid air, and he could feel a shiver wash down his spine. "Money?" she mocked, her voice dripping with contempt. "I am a walker between worlds, *darling*. Your currency is of little good in the dark realm, as you will soon discover."

James just looked at her, dumbfounded.

"You have but one chance at survival," the faux Molly offered. "I have another hunt to which I must attend. Should you escape this place and crest the hill from whence you came, I will release you."

"I can't even walk."

The creature walked toward the cave's exit and stopped. It turned around to regard James, and he watched in horror as its silhouette shifted in the moonlight. It morphed from Molly's small feminine form into a tall but gaunt humanoid shape. The monster had a hunchback, cloven hooves, and an impressive set of antlers resting on its brow.

"You will find a way," it grunted in a deep, echoing voice, "if you wish to live."

That said, the creature bounded away with a loud snort, its misty breath trailing off into the night.

James rolled onto his stomach and crawled over to the fire. He took a minute to enjoy the warmth of the flames before forsaking the only comfort available to him. He then inched his way to the icy den's exit. He pushed himself up to look over the stoop, only to discover that the cave was set into the side of a high cliff. James nearly gave up on life then and there, but he knew that's not what Molly—the *real* Molly— would want for him. She would want him to live. And she would want him to help his best friend.

Jonas took a knee and looked up at the sky. There was hardly a cloud to be seen, and the moon was almost full. His eyes lowered again, and he focused on the top of the massive slope he was climbing. He felt like he'd been walking forever, but he was only halfway there.

"Just a little further," he reassured himself, "keep moving, Jonas."

He heard a shuffling behind him then. He could have sworn he caught sight of a massive reindeer running by in his peripheral vision. When he turned, he saw something he did not expect. A short woman covered head-to-toe in cold weather gear stood a few feet away, facing away from him.

"Molly?"

"Jonas!" she called. "I finally found you! Please come!"

She motioned for him to follow and took off down the hill, back the way he had come.

"Wait!" Jonas yelled after her, "Where is James?"

"He's this way!" She answered, never slowing her run.

Jonas shook his head in frustration and ran after her. "Molly, stop! We need a plan! We need supplies!"

"Just come!"

Jonas was tired, and he was quickly losing his patience, but he trusted Molly. If James's situation was desperate, then he knew she would only do what was best for him. Jonas was an active paramedic for nearly a decade. Molly obviously believed his training would be adequate to rescue James from whatever predicament he was currently in. The lack of equipment would make that difficult, though, depending on the circumstances.

"Hey!" he shouted at her back. "At least give me the gist of what happened!"

She ignored his request and led him to the bottom of the slope, then stopped dead in her tracks. Jonas skidded to a halt just behind her. Molly pointed upward to a series of cliffs on the face of another hillside, about a mile off.

"He is there. He is injured. He will die there without your aid."

That caused Jonas to squint and raise an eyebrow. That sounded like a line from a dark drama. It didn't sound like something Molly would say. She turned to face him then, and the dancing red flames in her eyes caused Jonas to stumble backward.

"What the actual fu…"

Jonas dared to lean forward, poking a finger into her shoulder. "Are you… what is this?"

Molly turned and smiled. She leaned forward as well and pressed her lips against his. She embraced him and initiated a passionate kiss.

Confused and a little delirious from the bitter cold and the stress of the day, Jonas just went with it. He assumed she was similarly impaired and wondered if she might be suffering from a head injury. But those eyes…

"I know you always wanted me, Jonas." The creature purred into his ear, stirring him from his thoughts. "And James will likely die no matter what we do. We could leave him to his fate, leave this frozen hell, and get to know each other much more intimately. Like we always wanted to."

Too far.

Jonas pulled away from her and glared into her glowing red orbs. "Molly, what the fuck!? I don't know what the hell is going on with you, but this isn't happening. If James is in danger, we need to get to him. I'm not leaving my best friend to die while I fuck his wife! Holy shit!"

Again, Molly smiled wide. She licked her lips and looked him up and down.

"Crazy bitch," Jonas mumbled, shaking his head. He turned back toward the cliffs, reached for his binoculars. He searched the snow-covered rock for openings. He never even saw the needle-like claws pushing through the fingers of Molly's heavy gloves.

Jonas exhaled hard and let out an agonized cry when he felt the thin spikes plunge into his back. He jerked backward and looked down to see the tips of four talons protruding from his belly. He lurched forward, freeing himself from the piercing claws, and turned sharply. Molly was gone. There was only a small vortex of swirling snow where she once stood.

"What the hell!?" Jonas screamed into the night sky, wondering if he was losing his mind.

The persistent pain in his midsection reminded him that these events were quite real.

"I told you," Came a whisper in the wind: "Your friends are dead."

Jonas stood and twisted himself into a pretzel, looking around. He gripped his torso and retrieved an ice axe from his belt, anticipating another attack.

None came. Jonas found himself cold and alone once more, now in severe pain. He wasn't sure how badly he was bleeding. With the icy winds blowing ever stronger, he didn't dare open his coat to find out. Jonas turned to scan the top of the slope. He swiveled again to scan the cliffs where James might still be alive, then back to the hilltop. Through the swirling mist, he saw something that made his decision easier. A mammoth polar bear crested the bluff as he observed it, sniffing the air for its next meal.

"That settles it."

Jonas took a deep breath, picked up his feet, and fell into the rhythm of a slow jog toward his best friend.

He hoped.

James slammed his adze into the iced-over stone. He was halfway down the cliff's face now. The climb was challenging, to say the least, but the movement was doing him some good. His blood was flowing, and the sensation was slowly returning to his feeble legs. As his arms began to weaken, the restored use of his legs made the descent achievable.

He heard the echoes of a scream—a scream that sounded far too familiar for his liking.

"Shit!"

James wanted to pick up the pace, but that was impossible given his condition and the perilous surface he was climbing. All he could do was try to maintain his focus and continue his present course. Any misstep could spell disaster.

After what felt like an eternity, James finally put his first foot on the ground. He let his body fall into a slump, and he took a moment to warm his extremities and steady his breathing. After a while, he remembered the gravity of the situation. That creature could be anywhere. As he examined the vast white field before him, James saw movement on the terrain. A lump of gray trudging through the rising snow.

A person.

"Jonas!?" he yelled, his voice strained from a growing soreness.

James heard a faint sound come back—a reply—but he couldn't make out the words.

A violent current of air blasted between them, creating a blinding haze. That killed their attempted conversation before it even got started.

James pulled himself up and stabilized himself against the cliff face. He knew something terrible was about to happen. And he knew he needed to get to Jonas as soon as he could. James clenched his teeth and hobbled into the tempest.

Jonas was shocked to hear James shout to him from across the tundra. He called back to his friend just before a fierce wind cut between them.

"Oh, fuck you, fake Molly!" Jonas screamed, reaching his wits' end.

He gripped the ice axe tight and pushed into the arctic gale. The snow was piling up at an alarming rate. Jonas knew if he could reach James, they could put their minds together and get out of this alive. A few minutes in, Jonas could make out a shadow materializing within the white void. The shadow struggled to move and staggered toward him slowly. He shouted James's name but couldn't even hear his own voice, so he quickened his pace to reach the man.

Within a few feet, Jonas could see that it was indeed his best friend. He was hobbled and hunched over, using every ounce of his remaining strength to move forward. As they reached each other, James collapsed into Price's arms.

"Thank God," James croaked. "I... I thought..."

"Shh," Jonas shushed him. "It's okay, man. We're gonna be okay."

At that moment, Jonas felt a rush of heat and pain rip into the back of his knee. He cried out in agony, involuntarily dropping James to the ground before crashing down next to him. On his hands and knees, Jonas looked up at his friend, only to see a pair of fiery red eyes glaring back at him.

James let out a hideous laugh and brandished a bloody ice axe.

"Ah, you piece of shit!" Jonas screamed, lunging at the man with his own serrated blade.

The creature rolled aside, easily avoiding the swing. It continued to mock Price with grating laughter. It sprang at Jonas again, cutting a line into the back of his thick coat, then ran into the hoary curtain of wind.

Jonas shrieked into the white, picked himself up, and shuffled after him as fast as he could with his new injury.

James kept his eyes on the ground as he inched ahead. He'd occasionally glance up and around to make sure he wasn't being stalked. On one such occasion, he was stunned to see a screaming Jonas leap out of the swirling snow. He had both hands on his ice axe, which was coming down on him in an overhead chop.

"Shit…"

James was too frozen and cramped to dodge the blow. He managed to fall to the left, just enough for the saw-like blade to miss his head and plunge deep into the base of his neck. He could feel the heat pour out of him, covering his chest and arm in red. Warm steam rose from his body as he hit the ground, and he knew he had only a few more breaths on this earth.

He wouldn't go out alone.

"Fuck you, demon," James said in a whisper. It took every bit of strength that remained, but he tightened his grip on the adze and hacked at Jonas's chest. He buried the hooked steel between two of the man's ribs. He let go of the handle and fell onto his back, a delirious smile spreading over his face.

The force of the impact and the sudden pinch of pain caused Jonas to drop his own axe. He fell to his knees, straddling his prone friend. He looked into his eyes and saw James's brown orbs staring back at him, filled with contentment.

"James?" Jonas asked, a line of blood and spittle falling from his lips.

The look in James's eyes changed as they settled on Jonas's baby blues. His eyebrows furrowed, and a tear froze halfway down his cheek.

"Oh God, no…"

Jonas fell onto James, and together they succumbed to their wounds.

Their pain quickly turned to numbness. The numbness turned to darkness. The darkness turned into nothingness.

Then they both awoke.

Jonas rolled off his friend and stood up. James rose next to him, and the two took in their surroundings.

The sky was dark. Too dark. It was a curtain of black, not a cloud or star within the darkness. Likewise, the terrain was remarkably white—not a blemish—and all was silent. Not even their movements made any noise.

"Welcome," a ghostly voice echoed across the tundra, "to the other side."

An *inuksuk* stood tall before them, and they could see another further north

"Follow the cairns," the hollow voice continued, "or return to hunt... as *Ijiraq*. Choose."

They looked at each other, then looked beyond the *inuksuk*. There stood Molly. She wore a pained expression on her face but smiled at them through the sadness. She waved for them to join her.

Again, the friends looked into each other's eyes, and then they each made their choice.

THE SIEGE
BY QUIET RED

What they're in for is a world of horrors and a fight for their very lives against an enemy they can't possibly understand. The Rotten Man, as they call him, is not a foe to be taken lightly. In fact, if the prince's father were still in good health, he'd have given the terrifying thaumaturge what he wanted and spared his people the horrors of which they were soon to be subjected. All of this for some artifact. This artifact means nothing to the prince, his people, or the land, at large, and apparently everything to the Rotten Man. Yet, instead of handing the thing over, he's playing keep-away from one of the most feared individuals in the land.

The Rotten Man is known to some as a conqueror. To others, he is known as a reasonable man if one is willing to work within his demands. One thing everyone knows for sure is not to resist him. That brings only torment and malady, and the stories of the hellacious events the Rotten Man can rain down upon the unwilling are every bit the stuff of nightmares. Commander Moreaux has heard countless stories of the feats of necromancy that resistors have faced. Tales of cadaverous soldiers pouring into the gates, unending sieges that result only in his conquest, and graphic accounts of the fallen soldiers from each hold coming back to slaughter their former allies. Resisting the necromancer's power is a futile endeavor, and here they were, doing just that… for a useless trinket.

The prince's soldiers are brave—some of the bravest in the land—but they are mostly unaware of the threats they currently face. Moreaux watches them diligently perform their duties with pride and poise. Their pace is unrelenting. Prince Sedgewick has an army that rivals the size and skill of any army one could think of, thanks to his father. But even as Moreaux watches the men perfectly perform and prepare for battle, he is hit with a wave of melancholic dread for the knowledge of the fate likely to befall them.

Prince Sedgewick is holed up in his secure chamber, in the heart of the castle.

"Bring my father here, now!"

"We've sent two men to bring him, my prince." The servants make no eye contact, staring at the floor as they speak.

"Good. Make sure those locks are secure."

"We've checked them twice, my prince. They—"

"Check them again! There will be no mistakes made by you or anyone else in this keep. I'll not be eaten alive because of your lazy peasant disposition!"

Still looking down, the servant replies, "Yes, my prince." But inside, the servants and the guards around them can't help but despise him, for if he'd only give the necromancer what he wants, no one would be under threat of being eaten alive in the first place.

Outside, Moreaux is desperately making sure all the castle's defenses are in order. After making the last of his checks, he makes his way to the front wall to assess the situation. As he makes his hasty but somber walk to the wall, he reflects internally on the situation.

The prince is soon to inherit the throne from his dying father, and with that passing of power, the fears of the people will become very real. The young prince is well known for his lack of empathy, his temper, selfishness, and a penchant for snap judgments, not much else. In fact, it was the prince's dubious and shortsighted decision-making that put them in this horrible danger to begin with. Several bad decisions were made before the situation reached this point.

It all came about with an interaction Moreaux himself had with a peasant from the nearby village. One of Moreaux's men had escorted a common innkeeper to him, rambling about needing to speak to the prince. The man was disheveled and very clearly lower class, but he had a look in his tired eyes—something that compelled Moreaux to humor the man's rambling.

Annoyed, but intrigued, Moreaux listened to the commoner detail his encounter with an alarming-looking traveler. The stranger had come to their local pub looking for information. He was an intimidating man wearing a thick black hood with a scarf bunched around his neck, hiding much of his face. Stepping with a heavy foot, his broad shoulders carved a path through the patrons. He asked about an artifact—something he called the Psychopomp's Lodestar.

The traveler's voice was coarse and he spoke in the manner of an educated man. When he could see that no one knew of the artifact he was inquiring about, his interest in the whereabouts of the item shifted to details of the castle. The cloaked man asked about where the castle was, battles the army had fought in, who the ruler of the hold was, among other things. It was the latter-most question that stood out to the barkeep. This stranger was truly an outsider if he didn't even know who the ruling family was.

After the odd session of questioning, the stranger left, but not before the innkeeper caught a glimpse of his exposed face as he turned. The hood and scarf deformed just enough as he turned his head for the innkeeper to see a horribly scarred visage under the garments. This left no question to the commoner. That stranger was the Rotten Man. Anyone who knew of the Rotten Man knew that his face had been horribly disfigured in the backlash of a necromantic spell gone awry. Most say that he had been trying to recover the souls of his wife and daughter. Now he searches for anything that can help him in this endeavor, often taking whatever he's after by force.

Moreaux, however, was not entirely convinced by the tale, even if it was told with certainty and passion. Everyone knows the commoners love to work themselves into a frenzy with stories, especially those told with ale and wine. Still, something had gripped Moreaux's curiosity— the mention of this Psychopomp's Lodestar.

Such a title suggests the item would be of some importance, if not the simple fact that an outsider had shown up looking for it. If that was indeed the Rotten Man and he had come for something, then stories of his past indicate very few outcomes. With the name engraved in his mind, Moreaux took the information directly to the prince.

With his typical disgracious reaction, the prince told Moreaux, when presented with this information, that the item was indeed in his possession. To him, it was nothing but a trinket he'd acquired, from where he couldn't even recall, stating that it was probably among the items recovered from one of the numerous pagan sites the prince had raided recently. It meant nothing, and he was very clear. It was *his*. The prince took little from the information aside from a slight perturbation that someone seemed to want one of his things.

As it turns out, the Lodestar was an item of interest to the Rotten Man that happened to be in possession of the pagans. He'd made a deal with said pagans to acquire the item, but when the prince's men took it for themselves, they unwittingly made themselves a target for the feared necromancer. Not that any of those details would've mattered to the prince. Try as he might, Moreaux couldn't bring the fatuous monarch to take the situation seriously.

No more than a day later, the gatekeepers were hailed by a lone messenger. Granted entrance, the quirky loner presented a beautifully scrawled letter, addressing Prince Sedgewick directly. The letter explained that the prince was in possession of a valuable artifact, called the Psychopomp's Lodestar. However, this artifact was already spoken for when the prince acquired it. The letter concluded:

Assuming you had no way of knowing the item was spoken for, my dear prince, I would gladly excuse the inconvenience and leave peacefully, with the item in hand. If, however, this does not suit your own inclination, and you should choose to refuse this cordial solution, then more coercive means shall be explored. Rest assured, Prince Sedgewick, this refusal will result in copious amounts of cruor and anguish. Do the princely thing and save your people the horrors which shall otherwise be inflicted upon them.

Ever so humbly,
Charles Valencourt

This letter visibly infuriated Sedgewick as he read it, his face becoming more and more like a swelling cranberry as his eyes moved through each line of the parchment. Everyone in his court knew exactly what reaction was to be expected from the looks of him, and the foolish prince did not fail to prove them all prophets.

The livid prince crumpled the letter, throwing it at the messenger's feet, and exclaiming, "I will not heed an ultimatum given by some imbecilic lunatic! Listen here, courier, and take this message in response! I will not bend to anyone! If this '*Charles*' wants my things, he can pry them from me after he's pried the swords from the hands of my army!"

The messenger did not react, but simply stared at the ground. The prince made a final declaration.

"If this man shows his bloated face at my gates, he will be slaughtered and hung from my bridge as fodder for the crows! Now, leave my sight and my castle, and do not return!"

The messenger complied, but before departing, delivered these soft spoken words, "I shall do as you say, m'lord. But you shan't be averse to seeing the face of my master. You and your men will most assuredly be lost in the sullen faces of the bygone and the forgotten. Your house will see innumerable faces… m'lord. And you will pray to see that of the only man who can cease the hunger in them." With this, the messenger briskly left the court and the grounds, leaving behind a grim tension among the prince and his court, including Moreaux. Without so much as a word from his advisers, the prince had seemingly signed a death warrant for which his men would have to account. These decisions had snowballed into the situation at hand. Now, The Rotten Man had come to collect, pen in hand, blood in his inkwell.

Upon midday fading, the walls of the castle echo with the sound of a vociferating soldier. Moreaux is summoned to the wall to address the grotesque figure standing on the opposite bank of the raised drawbridge. The Rotten Man stands, wearing a long, tan sheepskin coat, trimmed in a dirt-stained white fur collar. His waist is garnished with pouches and salves, and his chest bears an intricate cuirass enhanced by unnatural features. His image evokes an essence of formidability and dread, but he is standing with only four other men—a peculiar sight to Moreaux.

As he looks on, Moreaux shouts at the man, "What do you plan on, with only five men, Valencourt?! You can't possibly believe you can overrun us with such a force!"

"You must be in charge! Please, call me Charles! We should at least be congenial, if not diplomatic, Commander! I will give you one last chance to end this without bloodshed! Hand over the Lodestar!"

"I can't do that!"

Charles ever so slightly pauses before responding with a stoic call, "So be it."

With that, Moreaux can see the necromancer repetitively raising his arms above his head. A slight viridian glow emanates from his body, which, no doubt, is some sort of dark magic. As Moreaux looks on, the wind seems to fall silent and the sun drops from the sky, setting night upon them. The Rotten Man says nothing. He simply holds his arms out, parallel to the ground, with palms turned upward—the glow of his magic now focused into his hands and growing more intense with nightfall. The almost peaceful display is suddenly interrupted by the sounds of violence from within the castle walls.

Moreaux is confused by the ruckus, as the necromancer hadn't moved, and neither had his handful of men. When the weathered knight finds the source of the sounds, he freezes, in awe. The royal crypt bursts open and pours forth the dead from within. Forgotten kings rabidly attack the now panicked inhabitants of the castle. The necromancer's power has begun its work. From outside the castle walls, across the boundaries of the moat, the devilry wielded by this man has pulled these withered corpses into undeath. The sheer power displayed here is like nothing ever seen by the people enduring it. He'd not even needed to breach the walls of their sanctuary to attack the men inside.

But the dead men within the crypt are finite and far less than an army. As the soldiers begin to fell the last of the putrid monarchs, Moreaux is invigorated by a realization—the Rotten Man can't get to them. This was nothing more than a scare tactic. After the last of the undead is put down, Moreaux makes his way to the wall to antagonize the necromancer.

"Charles, you must be joking! That was certainly a dirty trick, but nothing more! You'll find plenty more resolve where that came from! We are not frightened so easily!"

Inside, though, Moreaux and everyone else within the walls are fighting paralyzing fear after that display. His posturing may be forced, but he's confident in his assessment. So much so that he continues to bark at the Rotten Man.

"You've shown your hand, Charles! No more dead are inside these walls! Nothing more for you to sic upon us! And now we revel in your failure! You cannot breach these walls through this moat, and we will never lower the bridge! Your attempt to frighten us has only shown your desperation!"

Charles allows the echoes of Moreaux's voice to fade into the breeze, leaving an ominous silence in the air, before responding with a callous laugh.

"Is that right?! If you and your foolhardy prince insist on playing this out, then I shall begin my assault! I have no more patience for this standoff!"

The Rotten Man begins another spell of some sort, only this time, the ground shakes with an unnerving rumble. Charles speaks once more, this time in a hastened manner.

"Tell me—how many battles have been fought here, Commander?! How much blood has stained this soil over the course of history?! How many lay entombed in the earth?! You should realize that I have all the soldiers I need right below our feet!"

"You're insane, Charles!"

"Yes, and I'm tired of shouting! I shall speak softly to you very soon!

The Rotten Man nonchalantly turns and circles around his small posse of men. In one swift movement, he unsheathes his broadsword and brings it down with a swift slash. With a sharp flash of light glinting off the blade, he removes the head of the man in front of him. Despite the sudden act of violence, Moreaux can't help but take note of the blade the necromancer is brandishing. Even at a distance, the commander can tell that the weapon is a Templar's sword, but it looks to have the crosses and ornaments defiled and scratched away. Moreaux had heard stories that the Rotten Man was once a Templar, but like most stories about the Rotten Man, he didn't think it true. The order had been disbanded for many years and most were executed. Yet, here he was with what looked to be a genuine weapon of the crusades.

As the head rolls to a stop in front of them, the other men with him do not react to the occurrence, seeming indifferent, even hardhearted. Charles then raises his sword to the sky and forcibly recites an incantation.

"By blood and spirit, I call forth this malignant power to bring the dead upon my enemies! I shall repay in penance with death and supplant the risen with blood! Heed my call! Bare forth, undeath to my army!"

As he finishes the conjuration, the tip of his blood-marred sword begins to brightly glow with a subtle viridescent glimmer. From it manifests a vibrant skeletal phoenix that permeates the area around the necromancer with a viridian hue for several yards. The wisps of necromantic energy flickering throughout its ethereal skeletal form are nothing short of captivating to the amazed and disturbed onlookers. The ghostly construct takes to the sky above them before quickly diving to the ground with a stifled impact that emanates a visceral shock wave of raw energy, rippling across the hills, plains, and fields around the impact point.

As the rumble in the ground intensifies, Moreaux and his men begin to see burgeoning bodies emerge from the ground, across their entire field of view. Jagged, shambling limbs birth from the earth, grasping at the topsoil, raking with thin fingers. They rise in isolated spots before cropping up to pepper the land in smatterings. In seemingly no time at all, they turn to what resembles more of a spill of ink, dotting a black mass across a clear, pristine parchment. The land is dyed black with carrion. Such a sight is certainly a frightening one, but the sheer numbers are damn near maddening to the slack-jawed men looking on from the walls of the keep.

However, a few facts streak across Moreaux's nearly panicking mind. Firstly, the large moat still stands between themselves and the dead masses outside. Secondly, the Rotten Man has no artillery. He has no way of breaching the walls. Even if he had ten times their numbers, they could never make it inside the fortifications of the castle and the defenses of the soldiers within. Moreaux speaks to his men, rallying them and assuring them of these facts. The men are well trained and battle hardened, and the confidence of their commander is all they need to dig their heels in and follow command.

"Lock down those battlements! Get your hedge-born arse on the post, soldier! This is real! We're in for a long night, gentlemen. Lock it down!"

The gravelly shouts coming from Sir Moreaux echo across the walls loud and clear. Years of barking orders have made his lungs like a horn of truth to the men under his command. But underneath that strong, bravado-laden bellow, Moreaux is racked with doubt. He knows enough about their enemy to be afraid of what's coming their way. But he'd already beaten the ear of the young prince as much as any highly respected knight could reasonably do, and all to no avail, so Moreaux begins to formulate a plan. He realizes that fear cannot be allowed to sway his actions—that he must project inevitable victory for his men, if they are to keep their wits about them. That is until one of the men shouts to Commander Moreaux with a cracking, rattled voice.

The soldier is looking over the wall, pointing over the edge, finger shaking. As Moreaux peers down the side of the castle wall, his heart sinks as he spots a black mass in a section of the surrounding moat. Closer inspection reveals the undesirable truth. Moreaux witnesses a rotten mass of carcasses piling and folding on top of itself, forming a mound of bone and decaying flesh—a monolith of rot, and it's growing at a ridiculous rate.

In his dismay, Moreaux can muster no other words but, "My god."

As Moreaux looks on in disbelief, he breaks himself out of his awe-stricken stupor and immediately begins shouting orders at his men.

"Get the oil!"

Moreaux instructs his men to pour the oil over the edge and light the bodies. "They seem to think we don't know how to burn a body, boys! Soak that pile of bones and get those torches! Set these fucking things ablaze! Let's see how these rotten carcasses deal with the murder holes raining fire!"

One of the men hesitates in fear of the prince's retaliation for throwing the expensive oil down the murder holes.

"Sir, the prince told us to use the tallow only."

Moreaux grabs the soldier by the face and shoves him backward. "Get that fucking oil, now! You may face your death swiftly, at the hands of the axe, or you can watch as your entrails are ripped from your gut. I think you had best deal with the more immediate threat, soldier. Run!"

Moreaux's tone is gruff, laced with fury and fear. The soldiers frantically bring oil, arrows and torches, and begin dousing the mass of bodies piling up at the bottom of the castle wall as Moreaux's barks echo into the empty black horizon. Archers ignite their arrows and loose them into the writhing black mass, setting the reanimated ghouls ablaze.

The fire is abating their ability to stack, but before anyone can feel good about it, Moreaux, out of the corner of his eye, sees another jade glare flickering in the distance.

The nightfall has masked the necromancer, but Moreaux knows The Rotten Man is conjuring something. In a move of panic, Moreaux orders his archers to fire at the green light, hoping to strike down the source of this horror. The archers aim and fire. They watch the arrows fade into the distance, in pained anticipation. The emerald beacon abruptly fades and the light goes out.

Instantly, and without warning, a volley of blazing fireballs pour forth from the obscured view across the moat and heavily rain down upon the men with bone-shattering force and unimaginable heat. Moreaux and his soldiers are caught off guard, surprised by the flaming hell storm, scattering the men, sending them running in panic and falling over themselves to avoid the conflagration. Two of them are incinerated in a matter of moments by the mystical fire, the sight of which causing morale to take a sharp nosedive, and Moreaux can feel it.

The commander, solemn and fierce, riles his men once more with assertive roars and words of fortitude, managing to reel in the men just enough to stay their courage for a while longer. Though, for how long, he has no way of knowing. Moreaux quickly gets his men to take action. Lining up the archers, the grizzled commander orders his men to unleash a cloud of arrows in the direction of the necromancer. The men are firing blind, into the darkness, hoping to end this nightmare in one stroke of luck. Unfortunately for them, that wasn't to be the case.

As the men are still attempting to keep the pile of bodies in the moat at bay, Moreaux once again sees a glint of jade light but this time the light blooms to that of a large bulb in an instant, lighting the Rotten Man for a moment. In that moment, Moreaux stares into the eyes of the necromancer and they seem to stare back, glaring through dark orbs, mounted upon a hideous visage of painful looking decaying flesh. The sphere of energy hovers above the Rotten Man's hands and intensifies before slowly fading away like a dying torch, as the necromancer seems to flash a cheeky smirk just before fading into absolute darkness. Almost in sync with the glow of the necromancer's energy, the ruckus and chaos cease as the emerald glow fades, the night rings silent. All commotion stops and the dead men fall still. Moreaux peers out into the distance to behold no sign of the Rotten Man or his presence. It all simply... stops.

The sudden deafening silence leaves the men of the keep befuddled and mentally drained, almost as much as the attack itself. Moreaux realizes that the necromancer is simply playing psychological games, attempting to rattle his psyche and that of the defending soldiers. Recognizing the tactic, Moreaux acts swiftly, attempting to use the respite to prepare for the inevitable second wave of attacks before they begin.

The Gray Commander stations his men on active watch and hastily makes his way to the secure chamber where the prince is holed up. Prince Sedgewick is cowering inside the locked room with his father and several guards, along with the white priest, in the employ of the monarchy. All of them seem to be on the verge of pissing their pants, even though none have seen the terrors that have befallen the men outside the lavish locked chamber. In fact, Moreaux is met with a shriek from inside the room, as his knuckles rap upon the large door. He's certain it was the prince, but none say a word.

After making it known who he is, Moreaux is let in by the guards stationed inside the door. When he enters, he sees the prince guzzling wine, with a slight shiver in his hand as he purses his red stained lips to slog more back. The commander approaches the intoxicated Sedgewick and stands silent for a moment, awaiting the prince to acknowledge him.

"Moreaux! Why are you in my chamber? Have you murdered the villain outside our gates?"

"No, my prince. The necromancer has momentarily ceased the attack."

"If you haven't killed him, then why're you here?" The prince scoffs and rolls his eyes as he delivers the flippant words.

"My Lord, if I may take the priest to the wall…"

"The priest?" The two of them look over to the white priest, who pretends as though he doesn't hear their conversation, trying to appear preoccupied with nothing, but clearly hearing the commander's words. From the looks of it, he doesn't like them. "Yes, the priest should earn his station. Fine, fine. Take him with you. He hasn't prayed once since he's been in here, anyway. Find some use of him. Go."

"Thank you, my lord." Moreaux shifts his stance to face the priest and barks with his gruff, commanding voice. "Priest! Come with me." The priest seems to waffle for a moment, as if he is torn between compliance and cowardice. His head shifts between the commander and the prince, like a loose wagon wheel, but the expressions of the two clearly leave room for no leniency. Still, he tries his hand at worming out of the commander's request.

Delivering his last-ditch attempt in avoiding taking action against the necromancer, the priest pleas with a shaky voice and jittery mannerisms. "My prince, your father may need me if something were to happen."

The prince sneers at the attempt to use his father to manipulate the situation. "Do not pretend to have my father's best interest at heart. You have nothing but self interest in its place. Get out of my chamber!"

"Yes, my lord."

The priest shuffles his feet, head down, as he moves to the commander's side. Moreaux grabs the priest by the nape of the neck and applies a firm grasp, pushing the shuffling man along and out the chamber door. Moreaux berates the priest as they walk back toward the wall, stopping just short, inside a large archway.

"Listen, we both know you're no warrior. There's not a shred of courage in you. But this is not a battle that can be won by our men while you cower behind a locked door. We need your magic."

"Commander, I am at the mercy of our holy lord, just as you are. I am but a conduit. I can't—"

"You will! Conjure up the magic and the courage and help us. These men outside don't have holy blessings or magic wards. They fight because they have the heart to do so. Of all the gifts you've been granted, they have the one thing you can never invoke: the fighting spirit. They will fight, priest. You need only support them while they do."

With a slight sigh, the priest responds, "I… Very well, Commander. I will invoke the light to beat back this darkness."

"Good. Now, follow me."

Moreaux escorts the priest to the wall and parades him in front of the soldiers. Using the holy man as a beacon of hope, the Gray Commander invigorates the men with the sight of a possible answer to the dark magic terrorizing them. The tactic works, and the buzz of the men chattering in elation to the sight of the white priest begins to rally the forces. Moreaux instructs the watchmen to keep their eyes wide as the ranks of the keep surveil the nighttime vista, still dark with no sign of the dead or their puppet master.

The placid, cool air would normally be a preference for the sentries and watchmen, but tonight, the calm serves only as a harbinger of the chaos to come. The silence is uncomfortable and unnerving. Just as the tension and anxiety reaches a boiling point, a horn blows, bringing a chill to the spines of the soldiers. Never has the low blare of a horn cut so sharply through the minds of hardened men.

From the treeline, Moreaux faintly sees a handful of figures emerge and move toward the keep. It's the Rotten Man and his living followers strolling forth on horseback with no hesitation, coming right up to the edge of the moat, in full view. Lit by torches the necromancer's disciples are wielding, the men dismount and Charles steps forward to address the commander, who is eyeballing them.

"Commander. Shall we continue where we left off, or has your prince come to grips with the situation?"

Moreaux is so enticed by being able to clearly see the Rotten Man that, immediately after Charles speaks, he has his men fire in response.

"Your ruinous audacity does you no favors, Charles! Fire at will!"

The archers rain down arrows on the Rotten Man and his ilk, striking several of the men at his side, killing them. While the riddled men slump to the ground, Moreaux watches as the arrows simply deflect from Charles. Each one that strikes at him produces a sickening wail, sounding akin to what could be likened to the death cries of a torture victim. The arrows do no harm whatsoever. He only seems a bit annoyed by the aggressive act, glancing back at his fallen cohorts before turning slowly back to glare at Moreaux with an intimidating grimace.

What they don't know is that the sole piece of armor hugging the Rotten Man's torso is an enchanted cuirass, infused with dark magic. The Soulbound Cuirass, as it is called, is an ornate piece, looking as evil as the man who wears it, adorned with ghoulish imagery, sharp ridges, and rune markings etched into it. The surface of this ornate armor twists and writhes with faces of the souls trapped within, slithering across the surface in contortions of agony. With each blow against the necromancer, one of these souls is sacrificed to the void, taking the punishment in place of Charles. As grim as it is, it's quite effective, as no harm can befall him with this magical protection, as long as the cuirass is ingrained with the souls of the dead, and Charles has been collecting those for quite some time.

In witnessing this, Moreaux realizes that their previous attacks may not have simply missed, but that the attacks only bounced off. He stares into the face of the now antagonized Rotten Man, noting the ravaged and disgusting appearance of his decaying skin. He looks like a dead man himself.

"Looking a little worse for wear, Charles. Are you even going to survive long enough to win this battle?"

Charles scoffs. "Perhaps I have let myself go a bit too long. I've been somewhat preoccupied with bringing you to your knees, Commander."

Charles takes from his belt a salve—a potion of some sort—and pops the cork. After drinking the substance, the hideous decay and rot enveloping Charles' face begins to heal and fade away, leaving a normal, if not weathered looking man.

Charles tosses the bottle into the moat in front of him and looks up, scanning the men on the castle wall, before seeming to take particular interest in one thing. His eyes widen and he stares directly at the white priest, who is standing a bit further down the wall, surrounded by soldiers. Moreaux takes note of this, thinking that maybe the priest's presence concerns Charles.

The Gray Commander verbally jousts with Charles a bit more. "You're not the only one with magic on their side, necromancer. Tell me this—how does your virulent art fare against holy magic?"

Charles is visibly bothered, almost offended, and roars inflammatory words toward the priest. In a much less affable manner, Charles berates the man. "A white priest? Hah! Is this an attempt to befriend me with jests? Or are you just trying to warm my blood?"

"Your feelings mean little, Charles. This priest will be your undoing!"

"Charlatan! Endlessly projecting righteousness while you genuflect and shiver in the name of the colossi that tower over you. It must be a fantastic burden."

The priest is obviously shaken by the attention he's receiving from the infuriated necromancer, as he nervously begins an incantation, "In our lord's name I—"

Charles cuts him off with a gnarled warning, "Invoking your gods and their prayers will do little to curb my wrath, priest."

The priest feigns superiority, nose high in the air. Moreaux is taken aback by the newfound fury in the Rotten Man and urges the priest to ignore the necromancer and continue his work. So the priest begins his chant. As he does, Moreaux shouts to Charles.

"Our god holds dominion over us all, whether you acquiesce or not!"

Charles responds in kind. "Then I will set you free."

The confrontation with the white priest is a turning point in the Rotten Man's approach. All his mercy and whatever good nature may have been afforded are wiped away when, in his eyes, they defile his senses with the presence of a godly puppet and his pleads for deific assistance. Charles has the capacity to show mercy and benevolence, but his past relationship with the holy and all those who claim it have erased all sympathy toward such things.

The priest is diligently performing the incantation to bring forth his holy magic, reciting the words with purpose and further angering Charles.

"In judgment of my lord, my liege, the earth and the sun, powerful and righteous, I summon your warm light…"

The Rotten Man growls, takes a wide stance and points his eyes toward the ground, reciting a spell of his own. He speaks in a low, indiscernible fashion, in what vaguely sounds like another language, before raising his head, eyes wide and mouth agape. From them pours forth a black miasma that moves autonomously through the air, like a swarm of bees, heading directly to the priest and several of the men around him.

The pitch-black effluvium enters their pores and orifices, enveloping them and leaving the priest silent. Moreaux and the other soldiers fall silent as well and look on to what unfolds before them.

The afflicted men gag for a few moments, clutching and clawing at their chests. Suddenly, the white priest stops and drops his arms to his sides, before turning to one of the soldiers and grabbing a dagger from the waist of the man. He turns to Moreaux, looks into his eyes with a forlorn gaze, helpless in nature, and savagely slashes his own throat open with the blade. The guttural sounds from the priest vividly echo across the castle wall. The gurgling and grabbing at his throat as the blood profusely spills from the wound is a sight Moreaux has unfortunately seen before, but the look on the priest's face as he unwillingly takes his own life is new, and it proves haunting. It's as if he knew what he was doing but could do nothing to stop it.

In a similar, violent fashion, the other men meet their collective demise. Each of them murdering themselves, one after another. Some of the horrified men slowly shove pointed arrows into their open eyes, piercing them to the bone until the shafts snap. Others swallow their freshly sharpened swords, slashing their throats from the inside. As a crimson shower paints the stone under their feet, the men garishly maim themselves in various ways until all of them lay dead on the wall. Some of the other men lose all composure at the sight of these grisly events, and the panic sets in. Several more men jump to their deaths from sheer terror.

As the bodies of the suicidal men collide with the ground, the Rotten Man howls with a hearty, guttural laugh. Moreaux looks down at Charles with a chiding flare of his nostrils, completely disgusted with the apparent pleasure taken at the effects of the malediction he'd inflicted. The Rotten Man pokes at the commander, "I guess we know how my 'virulent' art fares against holy magic. Don't we?"

Moreaux responds in anger, "You're scum! How can you be so cold at the sight of lost lives?!"

"Cold? Commander, they are the lucky ones. They were spared abandonment..."

"What are you on about?"

"Time, Commander. *Time* abandons us all. The rest are left with misery and ghosts. You place far too much value on life."

"And you place none. I've taken my fair share of lives in my time, but I did it with honor, against men that pitted their lives against mine for what we believed. What you do is shameless. You sound like a man looking to justify his own vile actions."

"Honor is as pointless as any other ideal, Commander. We meander in this world, wallowing in our beliefs, just before we take a stride in the very footsteps of all those before us. We face the same oblivion. Cyclical. Voyeuristic. All for the pleasure of the powers that be. Whatever ideals you hold mean little to nothing in your blink of existence."

Charles takes a step forward and speaks even louder, ramping up his intensity. "I will not be fodder for the entertainment of faceless gods! The abyss has its talons firmly embedded in me, but it will *salivate* in foretaste until I have what I'm after! It just so happens that you've found yourself in the unfortunate position in between."

"What exactly is it you want, Charles? Surely there are other treasures you can take at a whim, with much less effort. Why here? Why now?"

Charles hesitates for a moment, briefly breaking eye contact and glancing to the ground while shifting his weight from one leg to the other, before locking eyes once more. "My family…" he said.

"I will humor you, Commander. I am a simple man. I once had a young family, a beautiful wife, and a perfect little daughter. They were my everything, my devotion, not some faceless ideal or god, but my family… and they were taken. On the worst day of my miserable life, I returned from hunting my daughter's favorite game, to find them dead, their bodies mutilated, not by animals or unholy spawn, but by men. God-fearing, righteous men.

"It dealt a blow more severe than any blade could ever inflict. So again, I rode for a hunt, and I found them. I slaughtered them. I slaughtered all of them, using the very weapon that fought for the gods—the sword you see at my side. I stained the hallowed blade with their warm blood in the name of something other than those gods for the first time, and it did absolutely nothing to slake my pain.

"I started dabbling in the dark arts, using my life's savings to acquire what I needed, and stole the rest. Many a court wizard found their libraries a bit less populated," said Charles, speaking with an air of levity.

The Rotten Man now paces the edge of the moat with uneasy body language as he goes on, "I had kept the bodies of the murderous thugs and I practiced on their corpses... obsessively. Eventually I was able to bring them back, and that I did... Then I killed them, again. I did this over and over... until I lost what little I had left of the man I was.

"Once I had become bored of my attempt at revenge and I felt that I could bring my family back, I worked up the backbone to try an advanced spell I had been examining, something called a blood hymn. Deep down, I guess I knew I wasn't skilled enough or powerful enough to make it work, but I had to try. I felt I owed them that."

Charles makes lively gestures with his hands as he describes his actions. His eyes are intense, with long bouts of not blinking. It seems clear to Moreaux that this story is not a lie. This is personal, and it seems to bring out a slight twitch in the eyes of Charles—a mad stare.

Charles continues, "The fated spell was buried within the one tome that instilled a gripping fear in me. The cursed book was written by an infatuated occultist, ages ago, bound in the flesh of his children and the pages marked by his own blood. Needless to say, the tome is not for the uninitiated. As it instructed, I had acquired two suitable bodies for their souls to anchor to our world. I thought I was ready, but in my inexperience, I lost control of the magic. I was caught in a backlash of necrotic energy, losing the souls of my family in the process. I cast their souls into the void with my own foolhardy attempt to save them.

"I have lived with that for longer than any man should, and I will live with it for centuries more, if need be. I have survived for nothing more than giving them what was ripped away. You see, this visage of mine, this... rot—it's not for nothing. It is a constant reminder of my failure as a husband and a father... as a man. And it is my penance to bear until I get them back.

"This artifact may help me do just that. So, you see, as I stated before, you've simply found yourself between myself and my family. And that's not a good place to be, for anyone."

Moreaux doesn't respond to the Rotten Man's words, but inside, he fights the urge to have a semblance of sympathy for Charles. Moreaux realizes that violence is ingrained in this man. His disregard for life has settled in firmly. There will be no reasoning with him.

While Moreaux mulls through the thoughts in his head and blankly stares at Charles, the necromancer points up at the wall. "You've got more soldiers for me, I see."

Moreaux realizes what Charles is referring to. The commander pushes off the wall, spins around and commands the remaining men to quickly dump the bodies over the side. The dead tumble from the heights of the stone obstruction as Charles lets out a light chuckle and turns to face his fallen companions. Charles walks over to one of the dead men and reaches down to rip out the arrows stuck in him. He kneels to place his hand on the dead man's chest. A brief but bright glow emanates from beneath his palm and the man gasps back to life. He does the same to the others who were struck down, then stands to face the keep.

"Commander, I have only begun. This back and forth has been enjoyable. I almost like you. But I will kill each and every one of you in that keep before I command your helpless shambling corpse to lower the bridge. I *will* have the Lodestar. In fact, I may just go find a nice place to dine while you deal with the problems I leave at your door." He lets out another laugh and turns to walk to his horse. He and his newly resurrected followers mount their steeds and ride out into the darkness once more.

Over the course of two days and three nights, the Rotten Man's necrotic magic lights the fields around the keep, intermittently flashing in and out, with the waves of each sudden attack. His army of dead ranks lay siege to the structure with unrelenting fervor. Moreaux and his men beat them back every time, but with each attack, it grows harder and harder. Sleepless nights, ailed with crippling bouts of anxiety and miserable night sweats, rack the men guarding the keep. Each one fighting the constant mental images of being torn apart on sight by mindless dead minions. Others continue to have mental breaks, remembering the carnage and death they've seen in the past several days.

Moreaux is vigilant on the wall, staring into the hollow darkness each night. As each wave of mindless gnashing teeth come and go, he uses every ounce of his imagination and mental strength to hold the night at bay. His prayers and wish-making are, of course, no use, though he can't help but attempt to free himself of this nightmare—to wake up and realize it was all just a dream.

The resilience of the men defending the castle is thinned to a sliver. Each attack from the breathless forces dwindles the will of every man still standing. Exhaustion is unavoidable, and rotating ranks is no longer an option. Too many have fallen. That of attrition is not a war that can be won against the dead, and Moreaux knows it. The initial hope—the naivete—is just as dead as the ranks slamming against the walls. All the while, the prince hides in his luxurious chamber, shielded from the horrors surrounding him. However, this detachment is not to last for the cowardly monarch.

As Moreaux is prepping the defenses for yet another attack, he is summoned by one of the prince's guards. The interaction with the guard is enough to set off the commander's internal alarms, sparking an immediate suspicion that it isn't good news. The walk is brisk, and as they approach the door of the chamber, Moreaux can sense the disarray.

What Moreaux sees inside the chamber—the sheer sight— it is enough to stop Moreaux dead in his tracks.

"What the hell happened?" Moreaux's voice is shaking, his eyes darting around the scenery, "Is that…"

The scene set before Moreaux is wholly unexpected. It is a sight that changes the circumstances so drastically that Moreaux can't quite think of a path forward, at least not immediately. There is a delay in answering Moreaux's question. As simple as it is, none of the men can bring themselves to speak up. So, the commander asks once more.

"What happened?!"

"The king," utters one of the guards. "King Oro—He… came back."

Moreaux finds that his mouth won't cooperate. It's hanging open like a fly trap. He gathers his senses enough to urge the guard to continue. "What do you mean, 'came back'?"

The guard swallows the lump in his throat and speaks on. "The prince had been drinking heavily and nonstop. He was oblivious… his father—the king—had died during the night."

Moreaux starts to piece the guard's trembling words together, "His sickness…"

"Yes, he finally succumbed. We tried to inform the prince, but he was so inebriated that he didn't seem to understand us. He made us leave the king in his bed, then told us to bugger off."

"Get to the point!"

"The king came back to life! Er–well, he was animated. Before we knew what was going on, the prince was—King Oro ripped out his son's throat and ate at his face. There was nothing we could do to save him."

"And what of the king? Where is he?"

"We had to, Commander…" The man stutters with what is undoubtedly the fear of consequences for killing a king. Even if he was already dead, regicide was no light matter for these men.

"Spit it out," says Moreaux, with an impatient inflection.

"The king came rushing at us, still dripping with the prince's blood. When he got close, we—*I*... decapitated him." The guard points with a limp hand and a forward nod, "We threw his corpse from the window. We did the same with the prince's body."

The guard stands with his eyes fixated on the ground in front of him. Moreaux, and everyone else, stand just as still. The room is silent and inert. Moreaux consoles the guard. "You did the right thing in dumping the bodies. As far as I'm concerned, the prince died of his own ignorance." The men look around the room, making eye contact with one another, but not speaking.

"Where is the artifact?" asks Moreaux. A couple of the men point him to the artifact in the corner of the room, behind the prince's bed. The artifact gleams with a golden brilliance of reflected light from its exquisitely baroque surface. Moreaux walks over and swipes the resplendent Lodestar from its ornate housing with a hasty, agitated motion, and turns to address his men.

"I haven't been sure of what's a dream and what's real for a day or two now. But I'll tell you this: We're sure as hell not fighting for a dead man. I'm getting us out of this nightmare."

Moreaux storms out of the room with a single-minded pace. As he barrels down the hallways, he hears the unmistakable sound of the watchman's horn. The next wave has appeared. Moreaux begins to jog. He picks up his pace a bit and before he realizes it, he's damn near sprinting full speed through the castle. *This has to stop,* he thinks to himself. *We can't lose one more life in the effort to protect this fucking thing. There's no monarchy to reward us for trying and no reason to resist. Hopefully, this necromancer will show mercy to the remaining men.*

Moreaux breaks the plane of the archway leading to the wall just in time to see the hordes forming, back-lit by viridian light. The dead masses march forward amid the intense flashes of magic from the Rotten Man. Commander Moreaux scrambles to react. He yells to the horn-blower to blow the horn and surrender. The men are all too willing to raise the white flag and be done with the nightmarish standoff.

Moreaux shouts out to Charles, hoping he will oblige the attempt at surrender. To the collective relief of the commander and his men, Charles does indeed acknowledge the gesture. The horde of the dead stops moving, falling completely and eerily still, and the Rotten Man cuts a swath through them on his alabaster steed. Riding from the back, the dead droves part as he approaches—a biblical scene to the defenders. Charles approaches the moat, across from Moreaux, and still mounted on his steed, calls out to the commander.

"Commander," he says with a nod, "Am I to expect your capitulation?"

"Yes. We will surrender the artifact to you, Charles."

"I'm surprised your prince came to his senses."

"There is no prince. No man will resist. I only ask for your word."

"My word?"

"Do not harm anyone else. Take the artifact and do what you will with it. It is yours and our lives are ours. Enough has been lost."

Charles pauses, as if to think for a moment. He notes the bags under Moreaux's eyes and the general state of the ailing men around him. He discerns the commander isn't lying or attempting a ploy of some sort.

"Fine," Charles says. "Lower the bridge."

"I will lower it, but I need you to re-kill those monstrosities peppering our fields." The anxiety is readily apparent in the commander's voice. He's clearly trying like hell to end the battle.

Before Moreaux even finishes his sentence, the dead hordes outside suddenly drop to the ground, completely motionless. The sight of which resembles a domino effect at a massive scale while the thumping sound of their bodies dropping carries across the stale midday wind.

"My men will accompany me. The dead will not." Charles' deadpan stare still sends shards of uncertainty through Moreaux's mind.

Moreaux, with his seasoned bellow that's starting to become raspy and hoarse from the unrelenting shouting over the past few days, calls for the men to lower the drawbridge. There is an undeniable sense of dread in this request, but the men are so incredibly drained that they can do nothing but trust in what their commander is doing. As the bridge lowers and the cranking mechanisms echo through the castle, the hearts of every man inside are on the verge of palpitations.

When the bridge finally completes its descent and plods into the bank on the other side, the Rotten Man takes stride on his ivory steed, with his handful of men following behind. The sound of the horse's trot is all that can be heard.

Moreaux is standing just inside the gate to the keep, awaiting the Rotten Man and his followers. He stands motionless, his wine-colored cloak dirtied and flowing with the breeze rushing through the keep from the open gate. The silver accents of his armor are tinged and dirty. He is holding the Psychopomp's Lodestar in his hand.

The Rotten Man approaches on his horse and stops just short of Moreaux. The commander looks up at Charles with a look of acquiescence in his eyes. The two remain silent for just a moment, staring at each other before Charles breaks the silence.

"I told you I would speak softly to you soon."

"Indeed, you did." The corner of Moreaux's mouth curls tightly in a crooked frown when he closes his lips.

As he speaks, Charles nods toward the artifact in Moreaux's hand. "I could've killed all of you and taken that by force. You know that, don't you?"

"I don't know whether to give you my gratitude or condemnation for that, necromancer."

"Either is but a meaningless gesture to me, Commander. Just so long as you know my will is the only reason any of you are left. I suppose that's the extent of what's left of my compassion."

Moreaux says nothing in response, almost as if he doesn't agree—

but he does. Moreaux knows Charles avoided a more direct approach to getting through the gate.

Charles dismounts his horse and walks over to Moreaux. His stature is imposing, seeming larger than what Moreaux had thought, casting a shadow over the grizzled knight. He stands over Moreaux, dwarfing his frame and looming with an overbearing presence that begins to make Moreaux uncomfortable.

"I no longer claim the title of knight," booms Charles, "but I can respect your character, Commander. You seem to be one who's deserving of that designation.

Charles holds out his large hand, a reserved gesture for Moreaux to hand over the artifact.

"Everyone that still breathes owes that to your rational mind, Commander. Take solace in that."

Moreaux places the glimmering Lodestar in Charles' hand and drops his arm to his side as Charles places the item in a worn leather satchel on his belt. The two men share a moment of peace before Moreaux pipes up, just as Charles is about to mount his horse. Charles stops and turns his head as Moreaux speaks.

"So, that's it? You just ride off with the artifact, leaving us decimated? Our king is dead. Our prince is dead. Countless good men are dead, and our keep is heavily damaged. We'll be overrun by enemies within a fortnight."

Charles removes his hand from the reign of his horse, standing still and facing the broad side of the animal. As if he decided not to say whatever it was he had in mind, he resumes mounting his horse and jerks the reign, causing the steed to let out a loud neigh and spin in place. He points the horse toward the open gate and breaks across the bridge, his followers calmly following behind at a normal walking pace.

As the Rotten Man rides off and his followers clear the bridge, Moreaux stands in the same spot, not having moved an inch. The breeze rushing through the keep rustles the commander's cloak and the flags around the keep, creating a whipping and cracking sound that echoes through the walls. Moreaux stares into the distance in front of him, stoically, not focusing on anything, but internally, he's an utter wreck. The feeling of hopelessness and desolation he's left with is tainting his triumph in surviving the ordeal. The options that lay before them are few and horrid. Death looms at every avenue, and the necromancer that put them here has left them to whatever may come.

"The Rotten Man has turned us into just another desolate chapter in his story."

With a solemn demeanor, the commander mutters, "Close the gate."